Though born into a wealthy Italian family, Leonardo Guerranti has not had an easy life. Sold out by the woman who bore him, rejected by his stepmother, he's learned to be tough and strong. Love? Not in the cards for him. His younger brother Mariano runs the family's banking business, but a sudden setback means Leo must sacrifice himself for the good of the family by marrying the daughter of a business rival. However, an unforeseen complication arises that threatens the alliance between the two families, and Leo can't allow that.

Talisman Broussard has grown strong through necessity when both parents died in a car accident. With no one to rely on but herself, she's risen to every challenge. Friends become her new family, and when one of them wishes to speak with the son she hasn't seen in thirty-five years and explain why she left him, Tali vows to help her.

When the irresistible force that is Tali meets the immovable object that is Leo, something's gotta give. He's got the money and the determination to get his own way in whatever he chooses. But he's never met a woman with the Southern brass that Tali possesses when she sets her mind to something. One way or another, sparks will fly. Will the conflagration consume them in the process?

A Soulmate For Tali

ISBN: 978-1-4874-3881-4
Cover art by Angela Waters

Published by eXtasy Books Inc

Look for us online at:
www.eXtasybooks.com

A Soulmate For Tali

By

Marfa Lara

Dedication

For my parents who instilled the love for books in me from birth.

For Larry, your love, support, and belief in me have never wavered.

For Barbara, the day we sat next to each other in Math class was the beginning of a life-long adventure.

Prologue

Leonardo stepped out of the air-conditioned skyscraper and into the summer heat of Midtown Manhattan. His driver pulled out from a nearby garage. The car stopped, and Leo graciously opened the back door for Emma—his efficient New York assistant as well as the woman he trusted to run the office. The driver greeted him as they pulled into the traffic of West 53rd street. "I hope you enjoyed your lunch, Mr. Guerranti."

Leonardo answered with a quick "Yes, thank you." He'd just spent two hours at one of New York's famous French restaurants having a business lunch with a former head of state.

Leonardo scrolled through his phone, deleting useless emails and flagging others to answer later. The tall buildings and endless traffic jams didn't hold his interest. Leo kept an office in New York because Guerranti Private Security and Investigations needed to show a presence there, but one city was the same as any other to him.

"Your three PM just texted me. She changed her plans." Emma rolled her eyes.

"What now?" Leo massaged his temples, sensing a headache coming on. He didn't have time for Astrid's games. As the daughter of Crown Prince Eugen Gudmundsson, she'd been spoilt beyond belief. If the Crown Prince wasn't his good friend as well as an important client, Leonardo would never have agreed to provide her with private security. "Did she cancel?"

"No, you wish. Photographers are waiting outside her

hotel. Security will take her out the back, in disguise."

Leonardo sank into the supple leather of his seat. It could have been worse. "Fine. Let the staff at the front desk know."

Talisman took a deep breath. From her position across the street, she'd watched Leonardo Guerranti step out of the back of his fancy car and enter the building ten minutes ago. He was taller than she'd expected. The casual blue linen shirt and cream-colored pants with the hems rolled up were a stark contrast with the black Bentley that dropped him off at the front door of the building. The woman with him, in her gray pantsuit and red bag, appeared a little intimidating. Tali inhaled a deep, sharp breath. The smell of cigarette smoke and car exhaust filled her lungs. It was now or never. She didn't want to stand there for one minute longer. Leonardo Guerranti didn't return her calls, didn't respond to her emails, and his people refused to give her an appointment. She *had* to talk to him, and he'd left her few options. Tali *had* to get into that building, one way or another, and find Leonardo. She fixed her braid and straightened her crop top.

Faking confidence she didn't feel, Tali pushed her chin forward and crossed the street. She opened the building's front door and marched straight to the front desk, as though she belonged there. Two stylish young women sat behind a massive wood-and-glass counter. One was on the phone. The other girl glanced at Tali, tilting her head to one side, as if she was an object of curiosity or something.

"Good afternoon."

"Good afternoon." Tali cleared her throat. "I was wondering if…Well if…Is it possible for me to use a restroom?"

"I'm sorry miss, but this is a private building. You can't—"

"Yes, yes of course you can," the other receptionists

interrupted. "Take the elevator to the twentieth floor, then turn to your left."

Could it be so easy? Talisman frowned. But why was the nearest bathroom on the twentieth floor? Oh well, best not to look a gift horse in the mouth. "Thank you." She gave the woman a polite smile.

She marched to the elevator and pushed the button to go up. Tali had expected some resistance. These people hadn't been so nice the ten or so times she'd called to make an appointment. From her vantage point, she could hear the receptionists talking among themselves. So, being naturally inquisitive, Tali listened.

"—Emma told us she'd be in disguise and to let her in."

"But what if that's not her?"

"Long hair, speaks with an accent, and dressed like that? That's her. But if you want to stop her, be my guest."

Accent? Who had an accent, Tali wondered. But just then the elevator doors opened. Tali moved aside to let several people step out. Then she rushed in and pushed the button to close the doors before the girls had time to change their minds. Now that she was in the building, she had to get through the second part of her plan—find Guerranti's office and wait until he had no choice but listen to her.

Next stop, twentieth floor. When the doors opened, she entered a modern lobby with light gray walls, black leather armchairs, and a wooden counter against the far wall. The man behind the counter greeted Tali. "Good afternoon, ma'am. Signor Guerranti's office is down the hall and to your left. He'll be with you in a few minutes."

Clearly, they thought she was someone else. Best find his office before they realized they were making a big mistake. There were three doors at the end of the short hallway, but only one with Leonardo Guerranti's name, so she entered that one. His office was plain by New York City standards. She closed the door and took a peek around. He had a glass desk with a large leather chair on one side of the room and two smaller chairs on the other side of the desk. Near a corner a round table with more leather chairs was situated. Both the desk and the table contained a computer and monitors.

Behind her, someone pushed the door open. Tali twisted around to find herself face-to-face with Leonardo Guerranti. She'd spent enough time examining his photos online to recognize the man right away. But Talisman was unprepared for the rush of adrenaline that raced through her body. He was beautiful, with a powerful presence that pulled her to him. His eyes…she'd seen them before, and she didn't mean in pictures. Her stomach coiled into a knot. She had a funny feeling that Leonardo was having the same reaction.

"You are *not* Astrid Gudmundsson. Who the hell are you?"

The strong, husky sound of his voice broke through the haze in Tali's brain. "I'm Talisman. Talisman Broussard. I've been trying to talk to you for over a month." Did she sound as stupid to him as she did to her own ears?

At the sight of the woman standing before him, Leonardo's heart pumped blood at full speed. The muscles of his abdomen tightened, his lungs constricted, and his suddenly swollen shaft pushed against the fabric of his pants. The top she was wearing left little to the imagination, wrapped around her large breasts. Her nipples hardened right in front of him. She had almond-shaped blueish-green eyes that sparkled like the ocean. She was talking, but he wasn't listening. He knew her, didn't he? Those plump red lips didn't stop moving. For one wild moment, he considered pulling her towards himself and kissing her.

"Boss, that's the woman that's been calling, emailing, and contacting some of our clients to get a hold of you." Matteo's comment forced Leo out of his thoughts. "*She's* the stalker."

"Wait. What? No, I'm not a stalker." The curvy yet pocket-sized nymph stepped back. Her long purple braid swung from side to side as she swung her head from him to Matteo, to Thomas, the other bodyguard, and back to him.

"Our cameras have caught her staking out this building at all hours of the day and evening," Matteo kept talking. "What do you want us to do?"

The girl extended both arms out in front of her. "I just wanted to know when you were here. Your staff refused to give me an appointment. How do you know I'm not trying to hire your services?" Her eyes pleaded with him, but all that Leonardo wanted to do was escape. There was something about this woman that spelled danger for Leo.

"Get her out of here." Leo tried to leave the office, but the woman pounced on him. She grabbed his arm, digging her nails into his skin. Leo savored a hint of her scent, a mix of vanilla and jasmine, before Matteo and Thomas pulled her away from him. "Call the police. I'm pressing charges."

"For what?" she shrieked.

"Stalking. And assault." Leonardo focused on Matteo. "Hold her in another room until the police get here. I still have to find out where the hell's Astrid."

Talisman was still rattling something about having a message for him as Leo left the office. Her touch had sent electric shocks through his body. He yearned for a drink, sex, or both. When was the last time he'd had a woman in his bed? That's all it was, he needed release. He'd been celibate for too long. This Talisman person was hot, and Leonardo could imagine himself coming between those full breasts. He raked a hand over the top of his head. Enough of that. She was crazy, and better left to the police.

"Here you are." Emma walked out of the lift as Leo was about to enter. "Astrid's not coming after all. She decided to let her father and you handle her security detail."

"Good." He entered the lift and made room for his assistant. "I only have patience for one psychotic female per day."

"Excuse me?"

"I'll fill you in on the way to the mayor's office."

That night Talisman arrived home and locked the door of her tiny studio apartment. She was worn out, dehydrated, and famished. This had been a day straight from the deepest pits of Hell. She'd never spent a day in jail. How could he accuse her of assault? She'd merely grabbed one of his arms. His goons did worse to her. They threw her butt on the floor, then dragged her to another room until the police arrived. Tali inspected her image in the bathroom mirror. Her hair was a mess, her mascara had left black streaks on her cheeks from crying in her holding cell, and she smelled like a public toilet. Thank goodness Mr. High and Mighty Leonardo Guerranti had taken pity on her and removed the charges the same day.

She'd take a shower, have something to eat, and sleep for the next eight hours. Tomorrow she'd devise another plan to convince Leonardo Guerranti to listen to what she had to tell him. If he was obstinate, she was more so.

CHAPTER ONE

Grinding his teeth, Leo counted the number of pedestrians crossing the busy intersection in front of his car. There weren't enough people in London to keep his mind occupied as Gianna droned on and on with wedding talk. Why were they paying for an extravagant wedding planner if she was going to keep bothering him about every minor detail? *Dio Mio*, this wasn't even a real marriage—it was a business contract.

"Leonardo, are you paying attention?" Leo's stomach coiled into a knot and he blocked the impulse to end the call. "I can hear you breathing."

Leo wrapped his white-knuckled fingers around the steering wheel. It was late, and he'd worked during the entire flight from New York to London. He was mentally exhausted, and the last thing on his mind was this elaborate wedding Gianna was putting together. This was a marriage on paper only. He'd never wanted to get married, much less stage this over-the-top circus.

"I'm listening." All Leo wanted to know was where to show up and when. He didn't give a damn about the guest list. "This wedding is because of your father's absurd demands. You can handle the details yourself or let the wedding planner handle it. You don't care about this wedding either, Gianna."

"Daddy insists on seeing your guest list." The soft female voice rattled on. Her crafty old wolf of a father required a who's who of the world's wealthiest and most powerful people at his daughter's wedding. Damn him to Hell!

"Have the wedding planner contact my PA." A jumble of cuss words fought a war in Leo's head. He craved punching Vincenzo Romano in the face. If this marriage weren't crucial for his brother's success, Leo would never have agreed to tie himself to a woman he did not love. Not that Gianna was a victim. She was walking down the aisle willingly in order to please her father. Leo, on the other hand, was between the proverbial rock and a hard place. He'd spent his life avoiding this kind of entanglement.

"I'm sorry, Leo. My father…" Gianna's voice trailed off. This wasn't her fault. The old man had spoilt her from birth.

"Forget it." Leo hated this wedding nonsense. Loud thunder roared and a lightning bolt crackled ahead, piercing the evening storm clouds. The streetlights flickered, and a monsoon threatened to erupt. "I have to hang up now, Gianna."

Leo should have listened to his assistant and gone home to Isola Rosalia. Still, instinct told him to go see his new offices tonight. His life had changed drastically from the time when he'd agreed to marry Gianna Romano six months ago. He'd never wanted to get married. Leo's life was about working hard and playing hard. But when Vincenzo Romano threatened to stop the merger of their families' banks and put his brother's career in peril, Leo was trapped in his scheme.

Pressure was nothing new to Leo—he thrived on it. But this was a different kind of pressure. Deep in his bones, he knew he was making a huge mistake by marrying Gianna Romano. But how could he look his family in the eyes and say no?

The powerful sports car stopped before a renovated building in the Central Business District of London, near Canary Wharf. His brother had convinced him to partner with him in buying the old building, prime real estate for the largest branch of Guerranti Romano Financial Group in Great Britain. The penthouse was ideal for the British offices of

Guerranti Private Security and Investigations.

Leo ordered the valet to bring the Lamborghini back in thirty minutes. He pointed his phone toward the glass doors, and they slid open. Inside the lobby, a world of Art Deco greeted Leo. Checkered floors, glass chandeliers, glossy surfaces, and polished wood. A crooked smirk curled his lips. What on Earth possessed his brother to put Gianna in charge of decorating the interior of a bank? Mariano had a legendary antipathy for Gianna Romano. He called her a spoiled princess, a socialite, and a media personality famous for the company she kept but with zero brains. Was this concession another of Vincenzo Romano's latest requirements to complete the merger? Art Deco wasn't Leo's taste, but the results pleased him.

"Signor Guerranti, this way, please." A short, plump man wearing a uniform with the word *Security* on his shirt approached him.

"And how far are the lifts?" Had they moved the damned lifts to the other side of the world?

"My apologies, Signor Guerranti.," muttered the guard. "Your wife is waiting in the employee cafeteria. She wanted a cup of tea, but—"

Leo grabbed the man's podgy arm, forcing him to stop mid-stride.

"My wife?" That couldn't be. Given that he wasn't married, the man must be talking about the crazy girl from New York. Two weeks had passed since the last time he'd heard from her—she'd stalked him for over a month before her arrest. Who else would go to the trouble of posing as his non-existent spouse? He should order the security guard to call the police and leave before she saw he was there.

"Yes, sir, Mrs. Guerranti arrived a quarter of an hour ago." The guard wrinkled his brow. "I offered to set her up in a comfortable office, but—"

"Tell me how to get to the cafeteria and return to your post." How had this woman found him here tonight? Did she have a tracking device on him? If she wasn't a nutjob, he'd hire her. Not even an arrest or the threat of longer jail time had persuaded her to stop her lunacy.

The employee cafeteria was at the back of the building. Leo stood on the open-door threshold, observing his latest source of distress where she stood, her back to him.

She'd lied to security. Leo would have the stupid man fired tomorrow. No person in their right mind would think that he, Leonardo Guerranti, would ever marry this screwball who dressed like a clown from a hippy commune. The purple hair alone blasphemed against refinement. He followed her long braid to the section of bare skin between her shirt and the long skirt, accentuating her narrow waist and plump hips. She might be psychotic, but she had a great body. Leo shut his eyes for a second. What was he thinking? She wasn't even his type. She was pint-sized with voluptuous breasts and a face he'd never forget, although he couldn't see it right now—heart-shaped, with round cheeks that showed deep dimples when she smiled. Not that she'd had a chance to smile at him when they met. But he had found a few pictures of her online later. Definitely not his type. He knew he ought to leave before she saw him, but his feet were cemented to the floor.

She swung in his direction. "Mr. Guerranti, you're here." Too late to escape. "Sit down and let's talk."

A cramp twisted his gut again. He moved aside. "Leave, Ms. Broussard."

She crossed her arms as if daring him to kick her out of the building.

"You have thirty seconds to leave before security throws you out!" He held the door open, glaring at the defiant young woman.

"We both know that won't be happening, Signor

Guerranti." The colorful bird pulled out a metal chair and plopped herself on it. Her musical voice, with her heavy accent from the American South, raised the hair on his arms. "Please, don't pitch another hissy fit, and give me twenty minutes of your precious time." She pointed to a chair.

"Why the hell would I do that?"

She gave him a lazy stare through almond-shaped aquamarine eyes. "I won't stop until you do." She grinned. "I have something important to tell you. You're alone tonight, and you have time."

Leo stiffened the muscles of his neck. "Speak fast, then leave." Rising, she stood in front of him and shoved the screen of her mobile phone in his direction. The blood drained from Leo's face.

He narrowed his impeccable eyebrows, intensifying his focus on her face. "What do you want?" His voice morphed into a low, deep growl.

"Your momma wants to—"

"I don't have a mother!" The bizarre creature confronting him didn't flinch.

"Agustina Rossi is your mother." A whiff of her scent entered his nostrils. Vanilla and Jasmine again, his favorite scents from the garden at Isola Rosalia.

"I'll allow you twenty minutes, but not here." He seized her lower arm, pulling her beside him. Who was this woman, and what did she really want from him? How was she connected to the monster who gave birth to him for money?

"Where are we going?" she whined as he dragged her. The tap-tap-tap of her shoes forced an involuntary twitch in his jaw. Was she wearing wooden clogs? Her perpetual assault on elegance rattled him.

"To my office. I don't intend to have this conversation in public." Leo found the set of lifts and pressed the button for the penthouse.

"How come your company's name wasn't listed on the chart outside the building, or by the elevators?"

He dropped Talisman's arm when they entered the lift and used the touchpad to punch in a code, sending them straight to the penthouse. "That's how I want it." Leo slipped his hands into the pockets of his jeans. He owned the best and most significant private investigation and security firm worldwide. Advertising was not his top priority.

Talisman tilted her head. "It makes it harder to find you." She chewed on her bottom lip like a rabbit with a carrot. Did she have a thought that didn't come out of her mouth as soon as it entered her pretty head?

"You ask too many questions. Now answer this one. How did you know I'd come here tonight?" The lift doors slid open. Leo glanced at his new offices for the first time.

"I showed up and hoped you'd be here. And I was ready to come back every day." Talisman rushed out of the lift first. "Wow, this is a glass maze. People must feel like fish in a tank working in this place." Leo didn't appreciate her judgmental criticism. "I hope the bathrooms aren't made of glass as well."

"Keep your opinions to yourself." He held open the door to a conference room. "The clock's ticking." She strolled past him, her damned jasmine and vanilla scent lingering in his nostrils.

"Even the furniture's transparent." She plopped on a chair and dropped her embroidered tote bag on the conference table. "Not even a picture on a wall, huh?"

"This is high-end furniture made of transparent polycarbonate, designed by a well-known furniture house in Italy." Leo's temples throbbed.

"Boy, you got taken!" She rummaged through her purse and pulled out her mobile phone again. "I hope you didn't pay a fortune to some fancy-schmancy decorator for glass walls and plastic furniture." She snorted. "Man, rich people love to waste money."

What the hell was he doing? "I don't give a rat's behind about your opinion of my office. What do you want from me? Should I have you arrested again?" He placed both arms on the table and leaned into her personal space. "You won't get a free pass, like in New York." He blasted each word with deliberate precision for maximum effect. Leo dropped his eyes to Tali's chest. That blouse did nothing to hide the fact she wasn't wearing a bra. He lifted a hand, ready to run a thumb over one of her nipples and see how quickly it hardened under his touch. Had he lost his mind? He pulled away and took a seat in a chair, doing his best to block the mental image of Talisman Broussard's naked breasts.

"Bless your heart, Signor Guerranti. You could start an argument in an empty house. We'll be here longer than twenty minutes if you keep interrupting me." She lifted the phone and wiggled the screen in front of him.

Leo compressed his lips, but a tiny fraction of the corner of his mouth lifted. His phone rang. The caller was his brother.

"If you answer, I'm adding the time to my twenty minutes."

Leo sent the call to voicemail. "Go on." He snorted like a bull pushing to get out of the pen.

Her eyes sparkled. She wrinkled her delicate little nose. "Your momma and I are friends. When I moved to New York City, she hired me for private yoga lessons." Talisman placed the phone back in her bag. "She's been looking for you for years."

He scrutinized her face. What was her angle? She wasn't here out of the goodness of her heart. Extortion. Agustina must want money to keep her mouth shut. "Did she have amnesia and forget where she abandoned me?" He slammed the table with his fist.

"Hush up! You can be mad enough to drown puppies, but

don't take it out on me."

One of Leo's eyebrows shot up. How dare she speak to him that way.

"Don't tell me to shut up in *my* office."

"Aren't you precious? That tone won't work on me." Sarcasm dripped from her lips. "Your momma didn't forget a thing, and she wants to tell you her side of the story."

"This isn't my first rodeo, Ms. Broussard. Go back and tell her to forget it. Your time is up." He rushed to the door. "Get this straight, I will never forgive Agustina Rossi for the simple reason that I never forgive people who wrong me. Good night, Ms. Broussard."

"Signor Guerranti, you're making a huge mistake." Those damned shoes tapped a Morse code on the floor. The colorful bird pulled on his left arm. "She doesn't want your money."

Leo yanked his arm and kept walking.

The lift doors opened as soon as he touched the button on the wall. Leo stepped inside and Tali barged in behind him. An avalanche of colors nose-dived in the direction of the floor. No sane person wore those enormous heels without breaking a leg. He stepped forward, and Tali crash-landed on his chest.

"I'm so sorry!" She pressed her hands against him and he wrapped her waist with his arms.

"You're insane." He devoured her neck and cleavage with his eyes. Tali arched her back and Leo caressed her soft midriff. She looked at him with those sparkling eyes that reminded him of the sea surrounding Isola Rosalia. He delved his fingers under her shirt, touching her smooth skin. Her scent intoxicated him like the finest brandy.

"And you're meaner than a wet cat."

Leo's pulsating length expanded, thrusting against her belly. She unbuttoned the top of his shirt, revealing his muscles and golden skin. He loved the blush on her cheeks. She explored his back, and he trembled with every caress.

"You're Michelangelo's David, but in the flesh." Her musical, velvety voice trembled. The lift door closed.

Leo caressed her neck, mesmerized by the arrested expression on her face—erotic and innocent at once. No one's eyes had ever feasted on him the way hers did now. She touched his chest with the tip of her tongue. Leo's legs wobbled, and he locked his fingers on her hips.

"What are you doing?" he whispered in her ear.

"Tasting you." Not a note of guilt or confusion.

"What makes you think you can?" he whispered again.

"I don't know." She looked at his face, and there was another bizarre moment of recognition between them, like the first time they saw each other in New York. *Oh, come on*. That sort of thing wasn't real. He was tired, that's all.

"I'm going to kiss you." He had to taste those lips.

"What makes you think you can?" Her blue eyes gleamed with mischief.

"Here and now, you belong to me." A burden lifted off his chest. The rainbow after a storm.

Leo closed his eyes for a moment. His engagement with Gianna was a business arrangement. Was he supposed to stay celibate until the divorce? They were meant to be husband and wife in name only.

"What's wrong?"

"Nothing." What if Talisman expected more than a one-night stand?

She took the decision out of his hands when she stood on the tip of her toes and stole a tender kiss. A feathery stroke of soft, warm flesh ignited a fire in his veins. She offered her mouth to him and he claimed it. He kissed her the way he enjoyed aged brandy…slow and sweet. Her firm nipples pushed against his chest.

She was ready for him. His erection pulsated, growing harder. What if he pushed her against the lift wall and pounded into her? No, that wasn't enough. He wanted to touch her, taste her, penetrate her slowly, and feel her orgasms with his mouth and fingers. And only then would he allow himself the ecstasy of release.

He lowered his head and whispered in her ear the outrageously obscene, sexy details of his fantasy. She blushed, letting out a gasp.

"If we do this, it's for one night. We go our separate ways tomorrow." He made himself clear.

"But your momma—"

He covered her mouth with his index finger and shook his head. "Moot subject. If you don't accept my terms, we leave now." He voiced a final warning. "I promise we won't meet again."

She hesitated. Leo's stomach churned. "Fine, I accept your terms."

Leo's phone pinged with a text notification. It was his brother again.

We need to talk ASAP. My place, in 1 hr.

It wasn't like his brother to be so pushy.

"Something came up. I'll take you to your hotel." He buttoned his shirt. Her face fell. "I'll collect you tomorrow and we'll spend the day and night together." The lighthearted sensation returned to his chest when she agreed.

His Lamborghini waited outside the door. Talisman examined it. She scrunched her nose and frowned. He opened her door, tilting it upward, and she jumped. "What is this thing?"

Leo chuckled as he settled a hand on the small of her back. "Come on, I'll help you get inside." Five minutes later, the Lamborghini roared to life as it joined London traffic. A blinding sheet of rain covered the windshield, and they were in the middle of a violent storm.

Tali wrapped her wet hair in a towel and poured a third cup

of tea. Her empty stomach grumbled. She ordered a steak sandwich from room service, which was a frigging expensive sandwich, too. She opened the drapes. London's skyline shimmered in the distance. Thank goodness the rain had stopped. She had a great view from her hotel room on the tenth floor.

If she had any brains, she'd leave tomorrow and tell Agustina the plan hadn't worked. Leonardo Guerranti refused to speak to his mother. He was an obstinate creature, but he was a damned good kisser. She pressed her fingers to her lips. She craved what he offered her. What if she told him she was a virgin and he rejected her? Was it possible to hide that? Bless her heart, what was she thinking? If he didn't want her, she'd go home to New York and keep living her life. Even if he became her first lover, that would be a one-time thing.

Her soulmate was out there. A man who cared about the world, who looked for solutions for climate change and other social issues plaguing the planet...a man like her father. Eight years had passed since she'd lost her parents in that awful car crash. Eight years that she'd spent filling the void they left in the world. Now she was betraying them, betraying their ideals. And for who? Leo, a man who belonged to the elitist class who controlled the world with money.

It was just one day, for goodness sake. She wasn't marrying him. She desired sex with a man who looked like a mythological god. Long, jet-black hair, glittering gray eyes, and a strong chin peppered by a messy beard. His tanned chest was as hard as a Colorado boulder beneath her fingers. That would be one fabulous day of incredible sex that she'd treasure forever.

There was a knock on the door. Good Lord, let it be room service. She unlocked the door and ran to the bathroom to wash her hands. "Come in!" she shouted from the other room. "Please leave everything by the teacup. There's cash on the table for you. Thank you." She opened the faucet and let the cool water run over her hands before using the little hotel soap. "I never know if I'm supposed to tip when I check out or when the food is delivered." She heard footsteps and the thump of the door closing. Well! English manners were way overrated. She dried her hands and wandered back into the bedroom.

"Hello, Ms. Broussard."

Tali let out a scream. "How did you get in here?" Why was Leonardo Guerranti, looking madder than a wet hen, standing in her room?

"Doesn't feel good to be on the other side, does it?" His frame blocked the door.

"I don't understand." A covered silver tray sat on the table next to her tea. "Did you deliver my food?"

"You're full of questions." He advanced in her direction. She moved backward until her legs hit the side of the bed. "Were you planning your escape?" His deliberate speech gave her the heebie-jeebies.

"Planning to escape?" What in Sam Hill had happened while she bathed and drank enough tea to fill the Boston Harbor?

"Don't repeat what I say. Answer me!" If his eyes could shoot bullets, she'd be dead. Time to take the bull by the horns, even if this bull was like three times her size.

"I have no reason to lie. I accepted your offer." She started to lose her balance, or was it in her mind?

"You're nothing more than a wonderful friend working to reunite me with my mother." His flat, controlled tone belied the danger behind it. "You stalked me for months, but after one kiss, you reevaluated and pulled the plug on your plan? A kiss awakens the sleeping beauty. What a sweet angel of mercy you are."

"Stalking you? I didn't stalk you!" Technically, sneaking

her way into his office when he didn't answer her many phone calls, showing up at another of his offices and pretending to be his wife so the guard would let her inside might...possibly...qualify as a tiny bit of a stalker in a court of law. Deny, deny, deny! "We settled this stuff earlier. What bee got under your bonnet now?"

"You're the bee under my bonnet, Ms. Broussard!" His deep voice transformed into a fierce command.

"You should leave," she stammered. He didn't look as though he was going anywhere.

"So soon? And what will the world read tomorrow morning on those sleazy gossip websites? Will you tell them I'm a terrible husband who left you three days after marrying you?" He crossed both arms over his chest. The muscles of his forearms bulged. He could snap her like a nutcracker.d

"I don't know what you're talking about." Gossip websites? She didn't read them, much less talk to them.

"Stop the act. Your story went viral. And I underestimated your deviousness." He wore an intimidating mask with the same ease as Jackie Kennedy wore pearls. "How did you know where I'd go tonight?"

"I'm not saying another word until you tell me what's happening here." Tali pressed her lips together. Enough already.

"I'll indulge you this time." He shoved the phone in front of her face. The headlines read *Billionaire Leonardo Guerranti, dumps fiancée, Gia Romano, for unknown American girl.* Beneath was a photo of the two of them coming out of Leo's office building. Tali shivered as she read further. *The Italian mogul and brother of well-known banker Mariano Guerranti, is reported to have dumped his fiancée, Gianna Romano and was spotted in London with his new wife. No comment from the Guerranti or the Romano families.*

"You think *I* did this?" She used the moment to slip by him and stand on the opposite side of the room. The man's efficiency in invading her personal space alarmed her.

He lifted one ebony eyebrow. "No, it must be the other purple-haired crazy woman stalking me for months!" All right, so he was no stranger to sarcasm. "You told the security guard the same story."

How did the media know any of this? Why would the press give a flying fig about her? "I reckon they're after you, not me. Your staff might have alerted the reporters. It could've been the receptionist who told me you'd left New York and were flying to London." She brought a hand to her lips. Oops, she hadn't meant to sell the girl out. Her mouth worked faster than her brain. What would Agustina think when she read this lie? "Time for me to hit the road, Jack." She'd pack and take off within the hour.

"It won't be that easy." In two shakes of a lamb's tail, he clamped five strong fingers to her upper arm. "How stupid do you think I am? You're going nowhere without my consent."

"There's no damage here. *I'll* blow this popsicle stand and *you'll* tell them it's one big misunderstanding." Tali pulled her arm, but Leo kept his hold on her.

"No damage? How do you think my fiancée and her family will feel about my colorful new bride?" His words pushed past the fog in her brain.

"You have a fiancée? Do you think I would have kissed you if I'd known you were engaged to someone else? You're disgusting!" She pulled her arm and he finally dropped it.

He narrowed his wintry eyes. "They named *you* as the source. How much did they pay you for the story? Was having sex with me part of the plan?" His long legs, clad in designer jeans and black leather shoes, trekked a path on the carpet.

"I didn't get any money." Who told the media? The very idea was laughable, to think any news media would believe the word of a nobody from nowhere like herself. Not the receptionist, either. Tali had made up the story when she arrived at his building so the guard would let her in. "It had to be the guard."

"Now you blame someone else. It's never your fault. Going after my family was the biggest mistake of your life, and I'm going to destroy you." He shook a strand of long, black hair off his face. The man resembled a battleship in size and menace.

"What are you going to do? Kill me?" Her heart hammered against her ribs.

His voice thickened. "*Dio mio*!" He slapped his forehead. "For goodness sake, I'm not going to kill you."

"You look madder than a wet hen and you're threatening me. It's fair to think the worst." Time to regain control. She closed her eyes and concentrated on her breathing. One...two...three... Tali slid to the floor, closed her eyes, crossed her legs, and rested her hands on her thighs.

"What the hell are you doing now?" Leo's husky voice broke through her concentration. Tali took one last long breath before she reopened her eyes.

"I'm meditating."

"If you're done with your hippy manure, Great Shaman, I'll give you ten minutes to pack your bags and come with me." He pulled out a yellow chair, plopped himself on it, and stretched his legs. "Two men are waiting on the other side of the door in case the voices in your head tell you to run."

"I'm paid until tomorrow."

"Plans change. Your little stunt created a PR nightmare for my family. I'm stuck with you until we fix it. We leave for Italy tonight." He uncovered the silver tray and sniffed her sandwich. His face told her it wasn't to his hoity-toity taste. "If the press finds out about Agustina, what will happen to her? Do as I say. I'll do my best to keep her name out of this mess."

"And you'll talk to her?" Was there still a way for Tali to reunite Agustina with her son?

Leo rolled his eyes. "Yes. However, you *will* regret it if you don't leave with me tonight."

"Are you always such a shark, or am I just lucky?"

"I'm worse. Keep that in mind."

"Wait outside while I change clothes and pack my bag." She pointed to the door. He left the room but took the key card she kept on the little table.

Tali changed into a long dress and a pair of sandals. She towel-dried her hair. She'f brought clothes for no more than three days. Packing took only minutes.

Leaving London with Leonardo Guerranti was both dangerous and stupid. But going back to New York meant losing the possibility of reuniting Augustina with her son. Agustina deserved an opportunity to meet the jackass to whom she gave birth so she could tell him her side of the story.

Tali didn't know this man. She felt like she knew him, but that must be her hormones going crazy. He was so damned sexy. Nobody knew where she was. She could be like one of those women who were living their regular lives one day but the next day they disappeared and nobody heard from them again. She was packed and dressed. Time to face the music.

Chapter Two

Leo rubbed his eyes. Fatigue was setting in. *Maledizione*! They'd been flying for an hour, and he'd spent half of that time reading his men's compiled report on Talisman Broussard. Leo found nothing out of the ordinary until her arrest in New York for breaking into his office. She was the only child of an environmentalist father and a stay-at-home mother who sold handmade things at craft fairs. The family lived in a tiny house in Louisiana. Her parents died in a car crash before Talisman turned eighteen. She'd moved to Manhattan, worked as a yoga teacher, and volunteered in different organizations. Poor as a church mouse.

Leo grunted and pushed back his chair. Now Vincenzo Romano, the contemptible bastard, had threatened to stop the merger of his bank with the Guerranti family bank. It was essential to have a private conversation with Gianna. If the transaction fell through, his brother's reputation as a banker was compromised. The Board of Directors would fight to push him out. That would spell disaster for the Italian economy. People invested their hard-earned money based on Mariano's business acumen.

He dialed Gianna's number for the third time, reaching her voicemail. She was letting her father manipulate her again. Leonardo dialed the old fox's number.

"*Ciao,* Leonardo." A crusty voice croaked in Leo's ear. "I've been waiting for this call."

"You can't do this, Romano." The dark of night paled compared to the dismal storm seething in Leo's chest.

"I can do whatever the hell I want!" The crusty voice broke into a coughing fit.

Leo scrambled to the bar. He unscrewed a bottle of cognac. "You know this isn't true."

"You embarrassed my daughter, but most important—" The old man heaved. "Most importantly, you embarrassed *me*!"

Leo's hands rolled into fists. "Let me talk to Gianna and I'll fix this." There was one person to blame for this mess—the crazy woman stuffing her face in his lounge.

"Fix it. *Then* you may speak to my daughter." Vincenzo Romano's brittle voice broke. "I've little time left, Leonardo. Fix it, or I'll die before the merger happens." The manipulative fossil ended the call.

Extinguishing one fire added fuel to another. What if Agustina Rossi sold her story to the tabloids? His grandparents had found Leo's birth shameful. They'd kept his parentage a secret. Leo was a child when he found out the truth about his mother. At that moment, he'd decided he would never forgive her.

Leo found Talisman crossed-legged on the carpeted floor. She held a burger with one hand while chugging a glass of orange juice. A slice of chocolate cake waited by her bare feet.

"I have a dining room in this jet. There's no reason to eat on the floor." She had given him the silent treatment after leaving the hotel, except to demand food. Not exactly Mata Hari, was she? Maybe looking like a tree-hugging, new-age snowflake was her trick.

"You know, we hippies don't use dining rooms. Too bourgeois." She bit into her hamburger.

Time to count to ten. "You're not grasping the magnitude of the problems you've caused. Nor do you understand the trouble in which you find yourself." He sat on a beige leather sofa. "That little act you pulled could destroy a business deal worth billions of dollars. Thousands of people will not only lose money, but they'll also lose their jobs. My family's reputation will lie in ruins."

Tali rolled her eyes. "Oh please, you're such a drama queen." She finished her burger.

"My brother and my fiancée's father worked for two years to merge our banks. This is a critical merger with far-reaching consequences." She paid more attention to the food in front of her than she did to him. He thought of a million things he could do to that mouth right now. Better yet, something she could be doing to him with those plump lips, like wrapping them around his shaft until he—

"Tell them we're not married."

Leo gripped the edge of his seat, afraid he'd give in to his darkest impulse. "They posted pictures of us outside my office building. You told my security guard you're my wife. Your behavior embarrassed my fiancée. Her father is furious. Thousands of people will suffer the consequences. But hey, as long as you get what you want, the hell with the rest of the world, right?" Talisman cared about Talisman first and last. She was making it very easy for him to do what he had to do.

"I'll talk to your fiancée. Tell her this was a misunderstanding."

"Over my dead body. You'll stay at Isola Rosalia until I fix the chaos."

Tali set the glass of orange juice on the floor. "I swear, you'd argue with a fence post. I don't give a flying hoot about your family problems." She tapped on the floor with her nails. "I *am* sorry for your fiancée. You don't love her."

Leo crossed both arms over his broad chest. "What's that supposed to mean?"

Tali scoffed. "Earlier you had three gallons of lust in a two-gallon bucket. How much can you love the woman and want to sleep with me?"

Luckily for her, she stopped tapping her nails before his last nerve snapped.

"I don't answer to you, *arcobaleno.*" She was correct—he was hornier now than he was back in the elevator. What if he raised her dress, lowered her panties, and took her on the floor right here, right now? She wanted him. He saw her glance at the bulge in his pants and noticed the soft blush she still wore on her cheeks.

"What did you just call me?" Tali frowned, leaning in his direction.

"*Arcobaleno.* Italian for rainbow."

Tali lifted herself off the floor. "What happened to the purple hair?" Her long mane was blonde enough to appear white.

"Why do you need such a big plane? Don't you care about your carbon footprint?" She shot him a derogatory glance. "You're helping to destroy our planet with this humongous machine." Her scornful remark filled his throat with bile. He'd relish bringing her down a few notches before this was over. "By the way, they're called temporary colors, Grandpa!"

A toxic pain snaked its way to his temples. She made him work overtime to ignore her petulant, judgmental jabs. "We will land in a private airport in Rome soon. From there, we'll take my helicopter to Isola Rosalia." And hopefully to his bed shortly thereafter. Spy or not, con woman or not, she was driving him to a point of sexual frustration he hadn't experienced even as a teenager.

"I guess a few more carbon emissions won't kill anyone. Except for the planet, of course." She examined the amethyst stone on the table to her left. Brilliant, more sarcasm. "And where's Isola Rosalia?" She grabbed the plate with the slice of chocolate cake. The movement made her breasts jiggle, pulling his attention away from the conversation. Did she ever wear a bra? "Hello? Anybody home?"

Leo braced himself for the oncoming barrage of questions.

"Isola Rosalia is a semi-private island near the Pontine Archipelago, off the coast of Lazio." These islands he called home weren't on most people's list of travel destinations. Tali squealed and grinned. *Dio Mio,* she was captivating. He wanted to hear her make the same noises when he thrust his cock inside her.

"I've wanted to visit the Pontine Islands since Agustina told me stories of her life there." Tali stretched like a cat. "What does semi-private mean for an island?" She stabbed the cake and devoured a large portion. Soon he'd have her on her knees, in front of him, taking him in her mouth and swallowing him the same way.

Leo cleared his throat. "I own half of the island. The rest is populated by families who have lived there for many years." This was his paradise. He could ship her off to a remote farm in France or a cruise in one of his yachts. Either of them would keep her isolated and under his thumb. Isola Rosalia was his home. He shouldn't take her there. Who was he kidding? The only place he wanted to send her was to his bed. How would those breasts feel when they were wet and soapy?

"Isola Rosalia sounds perfect. Do you want to know something?" She set aside the empty dessert dish and leaned forward as though ready to admit a valuable secret. "I've never told anyone before, but when I was a kid, ten or eleven years old, my mamma used to buy this coffee in a box. The box had a sketch of Venice." She held a distant expression. "I would think to myself *I'm going there one day because something special waits for me there.* I meant in Italy, not just Venice." She leaned back into her seat.

Was he now privy to one of Tali's longest-held secrets?

"If we're landing soon, I want to freshen up. And I have to call your momma. She'll worry when I'm not at the airport."

"There are three suites upstairs." He touched a button on the armrest. A flight attendant arrived. "Maria, show Ms.

Broussard to one of the suites, *per favore,* and clean this mess before we land. *Grazie.*" His phone rang. His father's name popped on the screen. "*Ciao, Papà.*"

"*Figlio,* what the hell is happening? I'm getting calls from the whole damned world regarding your wedding to an unknown American." Fausto's words burst out in a long-winded bark.

"Gossip, *Papà.* I will handle it." A sharp, cold dose of reality crept up Leo's back until it took control of his brain. He had to tell his father about Agustina, the woman who'd broken his heart and made a fool of him, who was trying to snake her way back into their lives. She'd been a maid in his family's home, and his father was the naïve, stupid heir who fell head over heels for the beautiful, sexy girl. His father fell in love, while his mother had been looking for a lot of money.

"*Si,* I know how you're handling it. Dragging the purple-haired freak to Isola Rosalia." He should've guessed Mariano had told him the whole story. "This is the same woman who stalked you in New York, is she not? You must send her away at once."

"*Papà,* I can't. Agustina sent her." Leo didn't sugarcoat things. "*Papà*?"

"She must disappear!" His father's voice thickened. "This will end in disaster."

Leo frowned. Fausto was a gentle person, even a doormat on occasion. At times the pressure of knowing how much his father depended on him to take care of the dirtier, more unsavory family problems was a heavy burden for Leo. His grandparents' ruthless legacy meant they'd made a lot of enemies. While Mariano managed the lucrative family banking business, Leonardo kept the barbarians at the gate. He'd find a way to mitigate this problem as well. Leo hated his mother. If she thought she could blackmail him or threaten his family to get more money, he'd be happy to show her the kind of man whom she birthed, then abandoned for a handful of cash.

Vincenzo Romano was a master at pulling strings. Stopping the merger of the two banks meant a catastrophe. Guerranti Bank and Romano Finances were two of the largest financial institutions in the world. Vincenzo had announced his retirement as chairman of Romano Finances and pledged his support for Mariano Guerranti to be his replacement. This union established his brother as one of the top influential men in his industry. During a private meeting with the Guerranti family, Vincenzo had announced another prerequisite for the deal—the marriage between Leo and his daughter.

Gianna chose which of the Guerranti brothers to marry. According to Vincenzo, he was terminally ill and needed his only child under the protection of a powerful family. Gianna chose him. Mariano had terrified her from childhood. Seeing her as a sweet and shy girl, Leo treated her like an older brother, whereas Mariano made it clear he considered her a spoilt brat and treated her with disdain when it was impossible to avoid her. He was the bane of her existence.

Leo had forged a secret deal with Gianna. They'd have a marriage of convenience until the passing of her father, at which time they'd divorce. Neither of them loved the other except as friends. They'd agreed to the marriage to please a cantankerous fossil and complete the blasted merger.

The weight of this ton of bricks on his chest asphyxiated him. After a couple of weeks in Isola Rosalia, enjoying his beach's clear, glassy waters, authentic Italian home-cooked meals, and laid-back atmosphere, he'd be good as new.

"Don't worry so much, *Papà.* I will do whatever it takes to take care of our family." He ended the call.

Tali wiggled inside her warm, fluffy cocoon as memories flooded her mind. *I'm in Italy.* She flung her eyes open. Bright light forced her to squint. The entire room was white and light gray. She rubbed her eyes and refocused. A jumbo-sized bedroom with two nightstands, uninteresting lamps, and a bed the size of Manhattan. What a total waste of space. Where were her things? Wait, what was she wearing? Oops, nothing.

Off to one side of the room, Tali spied a couple of billowy white drapes that diffused the daylight. She rolled her eyes. They must have a twelve-step program for people afraid of colors. She wrapped a blanket around herself and opened the drapes. With delight, she saw a beach in the distance.

"Her majesty awoke."

Tali spun like a merry-go-round, holding the blanket with both hands. Her mouth fell open at the sight of Leo. "What in the Sam Hill are you doing in my room?" She extended an arm and pointed to a door. "Get out, *now*!" He was wearing nothing more than a towel.

Tali narrowed her eyes, trying to identify the tattoo on his chest—an Italian flag and words she didn't understand.

"This bedroom suite belongs to me, and you're pointing to the dressing room." He approached the balcony. Tali scrambled back inside the room, tripping on the long blanket. She grabbed hold of the bed's footboard. "Ah...there's nothing like sea air." Leo took a deep breath, flexing his muscles.

She pressed her lips together. Whatever. She wasn't here to flirt with Leonardo. "Do you mind, you know...putting on your clothes?"

"Why so shy now? You didn't mind last night. You commanded me to do a striptease right before we—"

Tali shut her eyes. "You're a lying pig!" She thrust a pillow at him. He sidestepped it.

"*Madonna mia*! Take it easy. Nothing happened." He chuckled. "You'll remember when we sleep together."

"First of all, we're never sleeping together!"

"And second?"

"Second, I want my own room. And third, get dressed!" She crossed her arms. He threw his head back and laughed. Not one of his sarcastic laughs.

"Relax, Tali, you'll have your room. We arrived when the staff was asleep, so I brought you to my room." He opened another door. Tali saw a massive vanity with an arch-shaped mirror above. "I was going to tell you, but by the time I finished a business call, you were asleep. We slept on the same bed, but nothing happened. You still haven't said. Who is Sam Hill?"

"It's just a saying." She rolled her eyes.

"It's a man's name." He leaned against the wall, looking like the cat that ate the canary.

"For goodness sake, look it up." This had to be the stupidest conversation she'd ever had.

"Why? You can tell me now."

"He was a guy that used to swear a lot." Leo was a pain in the neck.

"And?"

"And he invented the moon. How the hell should I know?" Was she now supposed to be the expert on all sayings?

"You should know what you're saying when you say it."

"Really? You're going there?"

He grinned. "If you're going to say weird things, you should be able to explain them."

"That's not weird. Everybody knows about the Sam Hill expression!" She rolled her eyes.

"Maybe everybody where you come from, but not the whole world."

"Yeah? Bite me!" She looked around the room. "Where's my suitcase?"

"Everything's in the bathroom. I thought you'd like to shower and dress. Someone will come for you in an hour for a late lunch. And I *will* bite you, but not today." That said, Leo winked and disappeared into his dressing room.

Leo had a spectacular bathroom with an enormous walk-in shower, a soaking tub, and the fancy vanity she'd peeked at a minute ago. His shelves were stocked with luxurious toiletries for men, nothing for a lady. Tali sniffed at a bottle of cologne and smelled a woodsy, earthy scent.

Her things were near the shower, beside a wall rack with warm towels. There were showerheads, buttons, and a tiled bench. Time to figure this thing out.

An hour later, a young, uniformed woman introduced herself as Bianca. She led Tali through a catwalk with a view of another massive room downstairs. On both sides of the catwalk were two modern curved staircases with black wrought-iron designs. The cavernous room passing for a living room was furnished with stylish but dull pieces. Cushioned leather sofas and armchairs, glass coffee tables, and oyster-colored Damask area rugs. More white and gray everywhere. A floor-to-ceiling wall of glass windows showcased a view of a covered porch and a garden. Tali ran to the porch. Color, light, life!

They took a cobblestone path, strolling past white Jasmine shrubs and sweet autumn clematis with their vanilla scent and ivy-covered archways.

Tall oak trees shaded areas of the garden, flocks of birds perched on their branches. Tali was surprised to spy bananas, papayas, and even mango trees. Bianca stopped in front of a massive pink weeping cherry tree. A charming little round table and two chairs sat beneath the tree's blooming canopy.

Leo was feeding the koi fish in a pond. Dressed in casual jeans and a T-shirt, he appeared the most relaxed Tali had ever seen him. He greeted her like any well-mannered host.

"Here you are. Please, take a seat." He pulled out her chair. "*Grazie,* Bianca. *Per favore,* bring our food. We'll have a glass of wine while we wait." He uncorked the bottle of red wine and filled two glasses.

Tali did not trust this charming version of Leo. What happened to the argumentative, cranky beast? Best to sit, watch, and keep her guard as high as possible.

"How do you like my house, Talisman?" He tossed another handful of food to the fish before dropping himself on the other chair and taking a sip of wine.

"Your house is a lot like you." More in her element in this garden, Tali relaxed a little.

"How so?"

"Gorgeous and delightful on the outside, bleak and soulless on the inside." She regretted her words right away. Making him angry wasn't the way to get him to call Agustina.

"Perhaps one day you'll learn to be polite." He spoke in a dry tone. "Catch more flies with honey and all that."

"You're not a fly, and I'm not trying to catch you." Wasn't she, though? An apology was in order. "I'm sorry."

"I don't appreciate rudeness, but I do prefer people who are frank." He caressed one bunch of Black-eyed Susans.

"Was the garden here when you bought it?" That was a safer subject, hopefully.

"It was a plain bluff, ending at the beach. I hired local gardeners to prepare the land and create this place." He pointed to a blue wooden gate. "From there, it's a short stroll to my beach."

Bianca returned with a rolling tray full of silver dishes. She uncovered a garden salad, a plate filled with grapes and olives, a large bowl with tonnarelli pasta, and aromatic focaccia bread. Leo informed Tali that the chef had made her specialty, Pistachio Pesto. Tali rolled the pasta with her fork. She took her first bite, closed her eyes, and moaned with delight. "Oh, my goodness gracious, this is delicious!"

The food was too good for conversation. Leo looked sexy in those jeans and well-fitting T-shirt. Unlike the things she bought at secondhand shops or flea markets, everything he wore must have been made for him by a famous design house. She giggled.

"What's so funny?" He wiped the corner of his mouth with a napkin.

She thought fast. "It occurred to me that your house looks nothing like what I was expecting."

He raised an eyebrow. "What were you expecting?"

"I don't know. Maybe some prison-like place?" A fib, of course, but she enjoyed the little jab.

"Some prisons don't look like prisons but keep people under someone else's control. You'd do well to remember that, my little *arcobaleno*." He refilled their wine glasses and unscrewed two big water bottles.

Another thought occurred to Tali. "Are you going to fire the receptionist?" She'd been worried about the girl. What happened wasn't her fault.

"I don't fire people based on unfounded allegations." His flat tone and blank expression made it impossible for her to read more into his words. Did he think she'd lied?

"I never told her I was your wife," Tali insisted, in case he still had doubts. "She saw the police take me off in handcuffs anyway. She'd never believe it. I made up that story so the guard in London would let me inside." She'd feel guilty if that poor girl lost her job because of her inability to keep her mouth shut in front of Leonardo.

"I won't fire her, at least not over this one indiscretion."

Bianca returned to take away the empty dishes and brought dessert. Tali lit up at the round ricotta lemon cake. Bianca cut a piece large enough for two people.

"But it tells me there's a lack in my employees' training. In my business, discretion is of utmost importance."

Tali agreed with a movement of her head.

"I never saw a woman enjoy her food quite like you,

arcobaleno." Leo refused his dessert, enjoying a cup of espresso instead.

"You never met my momma." She pointed at him with her fork before sticking it back into the cake. "She could eat her weight in food every day. But we did lots of physical stuff, so we burned the calories. We gardened, swam in the creek, rode our bikes, and walked often."

Leo finished his espresso and stretched his long legs. "Looks like you take after her."

"I see a lot of your momma in you as well."

He straightened his back.

"I'm sorry. I didn't mean to make you uncomfortable."

"I don't want you to discuss my mother, at least for now." His steel gray eyes cut into her like the sharpest knife.

Behind his façade of cosmopolitan sophistication, she recognized his restrained but dangerous personality. His eyes told her volumes about his high intelligence. Leo's tall, athletic frame exuded an aura of fearless confidence.

"Bless your little heart. You're a hot mess!" She hoped her show of bravado would convince him. She wasn't about to let him see his threat find a home in her head.

"I have work to do." He pushed back his chair and stood to his full height. "The staff will help you with anything you need, within reason."

She'd called him a hot mess, but Tali was a hot mess too. When she lost her parents, she'd lost herself. She'd been a happy child, shielded from the world's cruelty. But that cruelty plunged her into adulthood before her eighteenth birthday. Living up to her parents' ideals and expectations gave her the purpose she needed to go on, to forge a life for herself. Her heart ached still, as if powerful fingers squeezed it in a vice. Why did she survive, but they didn't? She'd have preferred to die with them. Her momma and daddy worked to make the world a better place. One day she'd find her soulmate. Together they'd work to make the world a better place too.

Meeting Agustina was pure good luck. She never pressured Tali to talk about the past. She carved a place for herself in Tali's heart with nothing but patience and kindness. One way to improve the world was by helping her friend win back her relationship with her son. Tali used the rest of the day to explore the garden. She returned to the house at sunset and found Bianca picking flowers near the garden entrance.

"You enjoyed yourself today, *signorina*?" Bianca lifted her head and grinned. "Your room is ready. When you want me to show you?" Her English was broken but better than Tali's Italian.

"When you're done here is fine." The girl went back to work. "Why are you cutting those flowers?"

Bianca leaned close to Tali and spoke in a low voice. "It is *Signor* Leonardo, *signorina*. He told me to cut flowers and set them in arrangements. One for your bedroom, one for his bedroom, one for the living room, and one for his office." She rubbed her forehead with the back of her hand and kept cutting more flowers.

"He has a garden. He must like flowers. Don't you have fresh arrangements in the house?"

"My mum is the chef, *signorina*. We have lived here most of my life. *Signor* Leonardo never wanted flowers inside the house. This is the first time that he's requested them." Bianca grabbed an empty basket and her shears. "I'll be back in a few minutes to show you to your room."

Tali took another empty basket. "If you find me a pair of pruning shears, I can help you with the flowers." Bianca looked ready to protest, but Tali kept talking. "Two pairs of hands work faster than one." They went off together, chatting like old friends. It was easy to forget this place wasn't home. Besides, Tali strongly felt she needed a friend here.

Chapter Three

Leo rubbed his chin. His usual stubble was overgrown. He looked around the dark, expansive boardroom where he sat with only his brother and their father. They could have had this insufferable meeting at Fausto's house, but as usual, his brother was too busy to take a couple of hours off work. Leo glanced at the closed doors, wishing with all his power he could get up and get the hell out of there. He stretched his long legs under the table. Instead of water, the assistant should have brought them a bottle of whiskey.

Mariano banged a hand on the conference table. "How dare you question the word of *papà* now?" Hostility had been growing this morning in the conference room of Guerranti Bank's headquarters in Rome.

Leo bolted out of his chair and fixed his eyes on his younger brother. "That's not what I'm doing. I want to know how and why we are in this situation!" Mariano's obstinate, vicious temper poisoned the atmosphere. Leo crossed the space between himself and their father's browbeaten figure, leaning against a windowpane. "*Papà,* I'm not accusing you of anything. I'm asking you to think. Is it possible you forgot a detail I can use to nullify the situation?" He'd wasted three days in Rome trying to convince Vincenzo Romano to continue with the merger. He had to avoid many annoying reporters and paparazzi asking him stupid questions. They seemed to follow him everywhere, like pests. Leo was out of patience and on the verge of losing his temper. He was doing this all for his baby brother because of the guilt he'd been living with when he left the responsibility for the family business on Mariano's young shoulders. But Mariano was testing this guilt to its limits.

"Leave *papà* alone, Leonardo. This is *your* fault." Mariano's voice reverberated in the spacious room. "Did you sleep with the gold-digging slut, and now she's blackmailing us?"

A white-hot fire burned inside Leo. He fought the urge to punch his younger brother in the face. How dare he call Talisman a slut? "No. Call her a slut again and you'll need stitches on that pretty face." he bellowed. There was no reason on God's green Earth why it should enrage him that his brother vilified Talisman. She was the reason they were in this situation in the first place. But every cell in Leo's body revolted at the thought of his brother attacking her. He recognized a powerful, almost palpable sense of protection deep in his guts compelling him to shelter Talisman from danger. He didn't understand it, but he couldn't fight it off.

Leo was fed up with Mariano's behavior. For far too long now he'd had to change his life for his family. It wasn't just Mariano's business deal, or his father's demands that he handles the family's dirty little secrets, or the gaggle of relatives who expected the three of them to keep them living in the lap of luxury. It was that clump of emotions burning in his chest since the first day he met Talisman in New York. It confused him. It tortured him. Maybe if he just slept with her, he'd get her out of his system. But he wasn't about to admit that to his brother.

Mariano paced the room. "You threaten me over a woman who has been nothing but trouble for us? A woman who stalked you. You're putting her over *me*? Over us? I can't recognize you." That made two of them—Leo couldn't recognize himself either.

"Stop! Both of you, stop right now!" The deepening lines on his father's face were a punch to Leo's stomach. He hadn't meant to add to the older man's torment. "Son, Agustina sold you to our family. She took an enormous amount of cash and left the country. Motherhood wasn't for her. She signed her parental rights over to me. She blackmailed us, my parents paid her off, and she left." Fausto sat at the head of the long mahogany table, his shoulders hunched over. "If someone tells you differently, they're lying." His hands shook when he lifted a pitcher of water.

Mariano removed the pitcher from their father's hands and poured the water into a glass. He handed the glass to his father, then moved to the farthest corner of the conference room. "For once in your selfish life, put this family ahead of yourself." Looking like the wealthy banker he was, the younger brother confronted Leo again. "Kick her out of your house. Destroy her life, her reputation. I'll fly to the island and kick her out myself."

Beneath the appearance of a civilized man, Mariano was as fierce and dangerous as any mercenary working for Leo. No way in hell was he letting him near Talisman. "Don't even try it, *fratello.*" The men were ready to pounce on each other when the conference room doors opened wide. Gianna stood at the entryway with her little dog on a leash. She entered the room, closing the doors behind her.

"I heard your screams from out there." With her jet-black hair cut into a modern bob, clad in loose jeans, a red silk blouse, and wearing a gold bracelet, Gianna looked like an heiress. She graced the first row of major fashion shows and was much photographed by the paparazzi.

Leo frowned. He'd never paid much attention to Gianna's appearance. Mariano never missed an opportunity to remark on her looks, saying she resembled a store mannequin rather than a real-life woman. Worse still, Leo now agreed. When he left Isola Rosalia three days ago, Talisman wore a white top with pink ruffles, denim shorts, and flip-flop sandals. Dirt smudges covered her cheeks as she helped the gardener replant seedlings from pots into the ground. He wanted to take her into the cottage, strip her naked, and do everything he described to her in London.

Mariano grunted from across the boardroom. "This is a bank, not a dog park. What's that mutt doing in here?" The dog in question whined and cowered behind her owner.

"Gianna, we need to talk." Leo interrupted what undoubtedly would turn into a worse situation.

Gianna lifted a perfectly manicured hand. "No, Leo. I'm here because Fausto asked to see me. But it's as good a time as any to return this to you." She opened her purse and pulled out a little box that held the expensive engagement ring he'd bought for her.

Leo shook his head. "I want you to keep it. Let's work this out. At least hold on to the ring until we speak. Alone." Gianna put the box back inside her purse and Leo took a sharp breath. What was he doing? He really wanted to grab that ring out of her hand and toss it in the trash. That piece of jewelry represented more than losing his freedom. That ring meant the loss of something much more meaningful. His lungs constricted until Leo thought he'd suffocate. Gianna was speaking, and he forced his mind to refocus.

"I know you're not in love with me, and I put you in an impossible position by choosing you as my husband. It's just that the idea of marrying—" She stopped for a moment. "Anyway, I knew you'd agree, and that's the man you are."

"I'm sorry for—" The apology died in Leo's mouth.

"I'm leaving Italy for a while. We'll talk again when I return." She gave him a shaky smile.

"Gianna, *non puoi farlo*. You can't do this!" Mariano barked the command. Gianna cringed and the dog growled.

Leo rushed to Gianna's side as he always did when his brother attacked her. "*Va bene*. We'll work this out." He pressed her hand.

"Still saving me from the big, bad wolf." Gianna shifted her attention to Mariano. "I'm not a kid anymore." Leo knew she wasn't talking to him now. "I'm not afraid of any wolf!" Mariano grunted, and Leo smiled. "We'll talk again when this whole thing blows over." She walked over to Fausto and kneeled. "Papà isn't impossible, Fausto. He wants the merger too." She kissed the older man on each cheek and left the room as her dog pulled on the leash, happy to go.

Unwilling to continue this useless argument, Leo left as soon as possible. If he stayed, he'd end up in a fistfight with his brother, and over what? Talisman? Why did he get so upset when his brother called her a slut? There was nothing between Tali and him except sexual chemistry. He pressed the gas pedal of his Ferrari, cutting off other drivers. He had to get out of Rome. Why did he have this instinctive need to protect Talisman? Three weeks…they'd spent three whole weeks together on the island. And he'd found nothing that told him she wasn't the person she appeared to be.

Matteo, his friend and head of security, waited for him by the helicopter. Leo had wasted three days in Rome hoping to talk Vincenzo Romano into stopping his foolishness and completing the merger. The quarrelsome fossil's frailty hadn't diminished his strong will.

Leo hopped in the helicopter and buckled himself into his seat. Matteo followed him. Soon the blades went off and the aircraft soared. Both men secured noise-canceling headsets over their heads. Vincenzo's bottom-line demand was simple. Destroy Talisman's life and reputation. Gianna was his only child, and he spoiled her rotten. His American wife had died during childbirth. Vincenzo had become a loving but overprotective father.

On the other hand, there was Mariano. His concern was for the bank. At eighteen years of age, Leo had joined the military, leaving the bank on the shoulders of his aging father and younger brother. After leaving the military, he'd opened his security and investigations business and never looked back. The truth was that Mariano's demands were fair, and he owed it to his brother to help him get through this debacle.

As they approached Isola Rosalia, the colorful buildings perched on the side of a mountain came into full view. Boats bobbed in the marina, most of them fishing vessels. The copter flew over trees and pastureland where cows grazed in peace. Isola Rosalia had two personalities. The busy, bustling village on one side, filled with visitors and villagers making their living. The other side belonged to him. Leo had built his house on the peninsula opposite the village. He allowed the farmers to continue using his land for their cows to graze. That was the right thing to do. He had bought the land for the sole purpose of keeping it green and out of the hands of developers. The grateful farmers cared for the land as though it was their own.

Today his homecoming was different. To marry Gianna and complete the bank merger, he had to destroy Tali. He must shatter her reputation, show the world she was a stalker, a liar, a woman with a police record. He could get the ball rolling with a simple phone call to his Public Relations department.

Then there was Agustina. Growing up believing his mother had died during childbirth was painful enough. Finding out she'd sold him to his father opened a deeper wound that had never healed. He swallowed the agonizing knot in his throat. Agustina undoubtedly wanted more money, but she'd change her mind after the chaos in which he would leave her little messenger. The image of a pretty blonde with striking aquamarine eyes and clothes straight out of a hippy commune filled his mind.

"Boss, are you sure you want to do that?" Matteo had been

quiet during the return trip until now. "*Signorina* Broussard is not a person who would harm anybody." His bushy eyebrows formed deep wrinkles in the middle of his forehead.

"Are you forgetting your training, *amico mio*?" Leo and Matteo had joined the military simultaneously and had lived through things many people only saw in their nightmares. "I'm assessing this situation based on facts, not a pretty face." The helicopter had landed, and Leo unbuckled his seatbelt.

"Perhaps it is you who is forgetting your training."

Leo didn't appreciate Matteo's unwarranted opinion. He opened the door and hopped out of the helicopter. A warm breeze brushed against his face. "You have your instructions." A dip in the water was what Leo needed to clear his head. "Make sure the security team for the ambassador is ready to go."

As the sun dropped below the horizon, dusk painted the sky in blue, orange, and yellow hues. A riveting view of the sea welcomed Tali to the second-floor terrace. Amalfi lemon trees grew from large terracotta pots, expanding over a wooden pergola. The bright yellow fruit permeated the air with a citrusy scent. Two chaises under the pergola tempted people to sit back and relax.

This evening, a tablecloth covered the wooden table. Strings of lights lit the terrace. Yellow plates, pretty bright orange napkins, and a vase filled with flowers from the garden made the area look like the perfect spot for a romantic date, but this was not a date. What a contrast with the stark white and gray interior of the house. Tali nibbled on cheese and prosciutto ham from the antipasto platter. She leaned against the railing and stared at the green and blue waters of the Tyrrhenian Sea.

Leo had been hostile to her from the first time they met in

New York. He refused to listen to her. He accused her of breaking into his building. *Come on! That's one of the most secure buildings in The City.* She wasn't a cat burglar. She'd been friendly to the staff. They'd turned a blind eye when Tali asked to use the toilet. She found his office and waited inside. Five minutes later, he'd walked through the door with two other men. She recognized him, having studied photos of him online. He stopped in his tracks. They made eye contact. The pictures didn't do him justice. In real life, he was a splendid, manly creature with an aura of danger. For the briefest of moments, he appeared to recognize her. She felt that too. Had they met before? Impossible! She'd remember his rugged face and those bright eyes the color of hardened steel.

Five seconds later, all hell broke loose. He'd thrown a dying duck fit. There was a lot of yelling, and goons pulled her into another room. The cops handcuffed her and drove her to a police station. Luckily for her, Leonardo dropped the charges. She was plumb tuckered and looked like a ragamuffin by the time she'd made it home that evening. If that day someone had told her she'd be staying at his house in Italy, she'd have thought they were bonkers.

Tali smoothed her dress. From here, she couldn't see the beach. She did have a view of the white and gray volcanic rocks that formed Isola Rosalia. And farther ahead was the sea. The waves crashing against the rocks broke the quiet of the evening. Leo had been gone for three days, and she missed him. Silly girl.

Somewhere in the world a man was waiting for her, and that man was *not* Leonardo Guerranti. Her soulmate was kind. He cared about the environment and would join her in her spiritual journey. Her soulmate must be praying in an ashram or marching in an environmental protest, not flying the world in fossil fuel-guzzling airplanes or living on his semi-private island. This place wasn't her home, and Leo wasn't her soulmate. Her mission was to help her friend Agustina reunite with her son.

She grabbed the antipasto platter, sat on one of the chaises under the lemon trees and let the plate rest on her lap.

Leo stepped onto the terrace. "I apologize for my delay." He wore cargo shorts and a striped shirt with the sleeves rolled to his elbows. A half-grin tugged at one corner of his mouth. "I'm happy to see you didn't let yourself starve while you waited."

"Well, look what the cat dragged in." Tali jumped to her feet and placed the antipasto platter on the chaise. "You sure took your sweet time getting here."

"I'm a busy man." He pulled a chair for her. "Get used to it."

"I won't get used to rudeness, thank you very much." Tali wrinkled her nose and took her seat. "Lucky for me, I won't have to put up with it for much longer."

Bianca's arrival ended the bickering. She pushed a trolley with covered silver trays. Leo lifted one of the lids to reveal pasta carbonara, made with the fresh Italian black truffles Bianca's mother had brought in from the garden that morning. Tali's mouth watered. She gladly dug into her food.

"I never said how long you'd stay here." He opened the bottle of red wine and poured it into each of their glasses.

"I can't stay here forever. I've got a job and a life in the States." Tali rolled her fork in the pasta and allowed it to sit on her tongue for a moment. She closed her eyes. Heaven on a plate.

"Are you under the impression I'm giving you a choice? You'll be here for as long as necessary, *signorina*. Whatever you do, I'm sure it's easy to replace you." His words cut deep. People had said the same thing to her in the past, and she'd ignored them. But coming from Leo, those words hurt a great deal. She hunched over her plate and swallowed hard. *Stop it right now. You'll not cry in front of this man.*

Tali cleared her throat. "I know everyone is replaceable, *Signor* Guerranti, but I need my job." She forced another spoonful of pasta into her mouth. He had her trapped in his house for now, but Tali was nobody's doormat.

Chapter Four

Mariano's words echoed in Leo's head. *For once in your life, prioritize this family ahead of yourself.* Since taking charge of the family business, his brother had never complained. Never a word of reproach until today. Not that it stopped Leo from feeling guilty about putting all the responsibility on his younger brother. That ate at him every day. He'd inherited his mother's selfishness, which was one more reason to make his own way in the world. Had it not been for Agustina's greed, the Guerranti family wouldn't have been burdened by an illegitimate firstborn son. The bank should have always belonged to Mariano. He was the son born into a good marriage, and he was a better man than Leo had hoped to be.

Leo returned his attention to Tali. "I'm sure you've been paid well for our fake-marriage story, and you won't starve before you find your next target." She chewed her lower lip, still reminding him of a bunny. What if she was telling him the truth? Could he go through with his plans if her only sin was trying to reunite him with his mother? The report his staff had put together described a hard-working, innocent young woman. Too good for the likes of him. He stayed away from those women like the plague.

"There *are* no targets," she whispered. "I didn't sell any stories. Order your so-called world-class detectives to investigate me."

"They're working on it. What's your job?" He uncovered the tray with the lamb meatballs with Ricotta cheese he'd requested yesterday and dished some onto her plate. Giving them enough rope was the easiest way to lead someone into hanging themselves.

"You'll know when you get your report." She recovered her composure.

Tali picked up her food with her fork, but he noticed she didn't eat. This must be an act. Her big, sad eyes pierced him worse than anything she could say. What if she *had* told him the truth? If someone else sold the story to the media, they were blaming an innocent woman. Not just any woman, either. A woman who made him feel things. Things he'd spent his life avoiding. But then there was Agustina, the mother who abandoned him, the woman who sold him to his father. He would never forgive her….*could* never forgive her. He had no forgiveness in his heart for people who betrayed him. He'd deceived Tali to convince her to come to the island with him. Otherwise it would have been kidnapping. Of course she had agreed to go with him, he did not force her. Leo knew he was toeing a fine legal line here. It wasn't the first time the Guerranti family had toed that same line in the past. But he thought he was better than that. He thought he was cleaning up the terrible things done by his grandparents and great-grandparents. He would never hold her here against her will. If she demanded to leave, he'd let her leave. But she didn't have a snowball's chance in hell of achieving her ultimate goal.

If it were up to Leo alone, he'd let the story of how his mother took money from the Guerranti family and gave up her parental rights come out in the open already. Let the world judge Agustina for what she was, a rotten, unprincipled woman. But it made a difference to Fausto. He still held the values of certain old-money families. *Secrets stay within the family. You don't air your dirty laundry in public.* It was crucial to his father that Leo made sure this particular secret stayed buried, permanently.

Leo swallowed half of the contents of his wine glass. There

was another reason why he wanted her here. He wanted to sleep with Talisman until he was tired of her, as happened with every lover he'd ever had. But his family came first. Who was he to demand loyalty from others yet betray his family in their time of need?

"Are you always rebellious?" Leo examined Tali's features. She had pretty, chubby cheeks and plump lips. Pocket-sized as she was, the top of her head skimmed his chin when he hugged her. She wasn't a classic beauty, but she was alluring and shapely. When Tali smiled, her face beamed. Her dimples could charm the pants off any man…and charm him out of his money too. He'd dimmed her light tonight, and that bothered him more than he cared to admit. "If you don't eat your food, I might think the world's end is near." He tried to lighten the mood.

"I'm rebellious when I'm accused of something I didn't do." She didn't back down from a fight. Other women preferred to give in, knowing he'd reward them with an expensive trinket later. He liked her fighting spirit and her quick wit. There was more than a sexual attraction between them, much more. A deeper connection, but one best ignored.

"If you want me to talk to Augustina, do as I ask." He dangled the carrot in front of her. How many times would that trick work? He'd never talk to Agustina, but if lying worked, he would lie. Lying was how she got into his office and his life. He refused to feel any guilt for lying to her. She deserved a taste of her own medicine. In this case, as in many others, the ends justified the means.

"I'm a yoga instructor at a community center in Brooklyn" She paused as she stabbed her next meatball. "And I give private lessons in people's homes." Leo struggled to keep a straight face. This girl loved her food. "That's how I met your momma." She finished her wine and he refilled her glass. A little alcohol loosened people's tongues. "She paid for private lessons. I think she was lonely. Her husband passed away years ago, and they never had children." She took a long sip of wine. "They raised puppies instead."

He'd watched her practice yoga in the garden. She was terrific. He didn't want to hear another word about Agustina, her husband, or her damned puppies. "What do you want to do for the rest of your life? What are your ambitions?" People loved talking about themselves. He cut two slices of strawberry tart. She'd chosen a profession that allowed her to get into people's homes and personal lives. With her ability to show interest in people, to pretend to empathize with them, she could study her target well. What if she, not Agustina, had come up with the idea to find and blackmail him?

"You mean like climbing my way up the social ladder until I trap a rich man with more money than brains?" Talisman pushed her dessert plate away.

Leo furrowed his brow. "Funny for that to be the first thing you say." He bit into his tart. "Eat your dessert. In all of Italy, nobody makes *crostata alla panna cotta* like Noemi." He had to give her time to let her guard down. "Do you want to open a yoga studio?" So Agustina was a widow now, an easy target. She'd stayed away for thirty-five years. This had to be Talisman all along, pulling the strings.

"No way. You'll think my ambitions are stupid." She concentrated on her dessert.

Her peculiar comment raised his interest. "Try me."

"I want to find my soulmate, get married, have children, and live happily ever after." She took a bite of her tart. "There, I want the whole princess fairytale. Now I just need to find my soulmate."

"You're naïve, not stupid." Happily-ever-after was idiotic. Relationships didn't last, and marriages ended in divorce. Tali wasn't stupid. She was weaving her version of a fairytale, or spider web. This time the spider had trapped herself in her web, and he'd crush her like a bug under his shoe.

"I'm not naïve. My soulmate is out there, waiting for me." She raised her voice. "I know it, and I feel it in my bones. And when we meet, we'll both know it deep in our hearts. And your opinion is irrelevant." She was playing the innocent like a pro. Time to change tactics.

"You're right, *arcobaleno*. I'm too old and experienced for fairytales. My father gave his heart to women who broke it." He walked to the railing and rested his back against it. The silence of the evening allowed for the sound of crashing waves against the rocks to reach the terrace. A cool breeze played with his hair and refreshed the late summer evening, invigorating him. "Giana wants to marry me even though neither of us is in love with the other." Her eyes were on him. "Do I have a soulmate in the world waiting for me?"

The corners of her mouth shimmied upward. "Highly doubtful. The Universe would never punish an innocent woman with a ginger-snap rascal like you." Her grin widened from ear to ear. Whatever she'd said wasn't a compliment.

"A what?"

"A hotheaded jerk!"

Leo threw his head back and laughed. She wasn't the first to accuse him of being a hothead, but that was far from the truth. His training by the Special Forces of the Italian military had taught him strict self-discipline, but it was best for his plans if she didn't know that.

"And thank goodness for that!"

Morning light filtered through the soft curtains covering three large windows in Tali's bedroom. The room had the same stark white-and-beige colors as the rest of the house. But now Bianca had placed a vase filled with colorful flowers on a small white desk every two or three days. Tali rubbed the sleep out of her eyes and situated herself on the bay window seat. She drew open the curtains. From there, she had a partial view of the garden. On the other side of the bed, sliding doors opened to a small balcony overlooking the beach.

After yesterday's lunch, Leo had shut himself away in his office. He'd laughed when she called him a hotheaded jerk. His eyes sparkled when he laughed. There was an implacable streak in him, one that should scare her if she had the sense God gave a goose. Leo commanded power. He exuded confidence, but there was a softer side to him. Leo had excellent humor. He laughed at the silliest things, like when she tried teaching him to stand on his head. She was learning to recognize his moods by the look in his eyes. During those times when he allowed himself to be gentle, his eyes took on a softer color of gray. Leo was one of those people who smiled with their eyes. He also smelled good. Tali found that woody scent in his bathroom the first day, but with a difference. The chemistry of his body slightly changed the scent from what she smelled in the bottle. His golden skin was soft to the touch of her fingertips, but he was pure muscle. Not the huge, bulging muscles of bodybuilders. He was fit, outdoorsy, tall, and lean. In the elevator in London, he'd pressed himself against her. He'd been rock hard that night. Her insides contracted. Good grief, she was drenched just thinking about that. How she wanted him inside her now. What she wanted was sex, scorching hot sex with the sexiest man in the Universe. That's why she was here, on this island. She could tell herself a million times she was here to help Agustina, which was partially true. But the real reason why she'd followed along with his plan for her stay on this island, in his home, was for the opportunity to sleep with him.

Who cared if her first lover didn't love her? He was not just any lover, either. He was Leonardo Guerranti. When they did finally meet, her soulmate wouldn't care if she wasn't a virgin. Would Leo care that she was? What if finding out she was a virgin diminished his desire for her? Her knowledge of sex was theoretical. In practice, she had no idea what to do to please a man like him, a man who had his pick of the world's most beautiful and sophisticated women.

The real possibility of Leo turning her down because she was still a virgin at twenty-six became a deflating and eye-opening thought. She rubbed a hand over her face. *Come on, Tali!* She wasn't a rich and famous model who draped over Leo in photos like a cheap coat. He'd sleep with her if she let him, because she was a woman and available. Then he'd forget her the minute she stopped being a nuisance. He'd probably been in another woman's bed when he left her alone on the island. She took a deep breath, ignoring the sensation of elephants dancing on her chest. If he was a man-whore, that wasn't her problem. The irony of the situation didn't escape her. Who was she to judge him when she wanted to have sex with him, then go back to New York as if nothing had happened? A knock at the door brought her back to reality.

"Come in!" She covered herself with the blanket, disappointed to see it was only Bianca.

"*Buongiorno, signorina.*" Bianca smiled. "*Signor* Guerranti would like you to join him for breakfast in one hour. He said for you to wear *pantaloni.*" The girl giggled.

"*Pantaloni*? Like jeans?"

"*Si, signorina,* jeans." Bianca nodded. "I will go prepare your *bagno.*" She thought for a moment. "Your…bath, *si*?"

"No, you don't have to do that." The girl flashed Tali a quizzical look. Was she used to waiting hand and foot on Leo's women? Tali jumped out of bed. "I will prepare my bath, *grazie.*"

Did Leo think he just had to snap his fingers and she'd do whatever he ordered? One hour indeed. Bless his little black heart. His elevator wasn't going to the top floor this morning.

After dismissing Bianca, Tali rummaged through her bag. Time to shock the heck out of Mr. Wonderful today. Knowing Leo wouldn't have a problem walking into her bathroom, Tali locked the bedroom door.

It was going to take more than one hour to get herself ready. Let Leo wait, or he could eat without her. She let the water run in the soaking tub. Her mamma would've loved this bathtub. She dreamed of exchanging the tiny tub in their one bathroom for one of these fancy-schmancy types. But they never had the money for such luxuries. Her parents cared about people, not money. They volunteered to build houses for needy people, fed the hungry, and had a sofa for any friend in need, but they struggled to make ends meet. What would they think of her now? She was living in the lap of luxury, entertaining the idea of having an affair with a bossy member of the one-percent class.

Leonardo Guerranti's exclusive priorities were money and pleasure. He and Tali had nothing in common besides a deep sexual attraction. She was betraying herself and how her parents raised her if she allowed lust to change the path she set for her life. Leo wasn't good for her. He would hurt her, and she'd had enough pain in her life. She had to choose between betraying her parents or acting selfishly and going after what she wanted.

Chapter Five

"*Madonna mia,* what are you wearing now?" She'd kept him waiting for two hours. Now he saw why. She'd chosen to wear distressed jeans with more frays, holes, and tears than fabric, and another cropped top. One of those off-the-shoulder things. Her bare midriff showed off a pierced belly button. But her hair! Leo scraped a hand over his face. She'd dyed it pink-and-green, then styled it in messy dread-locks and feathers. Were those beads glued to her face? He was not going to react. Time to count to ten. She'd win if he acted on instinct and ordered her to change her clothes. She wanted to torment him—he'd walk over hot coals before he'd let that happen.

"I'm wearing pants, as you so graciously requested." She stepped off the bottom step and twirled. With a glimmer in her eyes, she defied him to complain. "I'm starving. Are we eating in the garden again?"

Leo shook his head. "If you're hungry, that's your fault." She winked and his anger evaporated. She'd been here for close to a month and had never once been outside the property. They spent time at the beach or the pool when he was home. In the evenings, they'd watch TV or play board games. "We're going to the village to eat at one of the *trattorias.* Would you like that?"

"Yes, very much!" She walked ahead, giving him a full view of her backside. And what a backside it was. They mounted his Vespa and took his private road, which hugged the coast for a while, then went up the cliffside, ending where it joined the main street leading to the village of Santa Rosalia. The two-lane route offered picturesque views of the ocean and the colorful fishing village perched on the side of a hill.

This morning he'd had an early call from his assistant. Agustina had gone to his office in New York and asked to speak to him. Of course, nobody there knew who she was, but he had people following her twenty-four hours a day. Leo had covered all his bases. She had to be concerned. She hadn't heard from Tali in a month. Should he let them speak again? If Agustina went to the media right now, what proof did she have? He'd squash her like a bug. Everyone would think it was another fake story, like his supposed marriage to Talisman. She'd still get money out of it, but nowhere near as much as she imagined she could get by blackmailing his family. No, he had to manipulate Tali into holding Agustina back until the merger happened. And for the merger to take place, he had to either marry Gianna or find a way to pressure her father into signing on the proverbial dotted line. Why hadn't he thought about that sooner? Vincenzo Romano must have a few skeletons in his closet. It was just a matter of finding them and using them to put enough pressure on him.

Leo slowed his Vespa as he maneuvered the narrow curve of the road hugging the coast. Tali's arms around his waist sent a rush of heat to his crotch. Leo parked by the side of the road and removed his helmet.

"Why are we stopping here?"

"To enjoy the view." They were halfway to the village. "Let's sit over there." He pointed to a fallen tree between the road and a strip of empty beach. "This is my favorite view of Isola Rosalia." He pointed at the marina below and the colorful building perched on the hillside. An assortment of small and midsize boats alongside canoes and other watercrafts were tied to several piers. The water reflected many shades of blue.

Tali examined the curve Leo had maneuvered. "The road is so narrow."

"I ride motorcycles, scooters, or even bicycles. There's a wider, safer street from the house to the village." He'd never brought a lover to this place, so why her? This girl was a threat. She knew about Agustina. He had to destroy her. But he was tearing himself apart by this undertaking. This was crazy. He should protect his family, but a primal instinct held him back.

"If I lived here, I'd never want to leave. This island is a tiny piece of paradise." She closed her eyes and breathed the salty air.

Until he met her, Leo had preferred to work long hours and enjoy the fruit of his success. Lavish parties, beautiful women, skydiving, skiing, car racing—anything and everything his heart desired. The adrenaline rush made him feel alive. The money and success proved to the world and himself that he was worthy of his last name. All of that changed when he'd brought Talisman here. Now he looked forward to coming home and watching TV with her or listening to her ideas for redecorating his house. Tali called the place a blank slate. She was right.

"Pretend you live here and enjoy it." He liked having Tali at Isola Rosalia, which was dangerous because she'd soon have to leave for good.

"When your momma told me the stories of her life growing up in these islands, I imagined the beauty of this place, but seeing it in person is way better." They sat next to each other on the tree trunk. He removed his shoes and dug his toes in the powdery sand.

"Agustina didn't set foot on Isola Rosalia and never will."

A scowl creased her forehead.

He allowed a cheeky grin to lighten his expression. "I'm sorry, Tali. Remember that I promised to talk to my mother, nothing else." He softened his tone.

"That's how you feel right now. But keep an open mind, please. Agustina is a kind woman, and she loves you." She reached out to touch his hand but stopped midair and let it rest on the tree trunk instead. "You need her in your life as much as she needs you."

A softer, naïve man might have fallen for her wide-eyed expression, but not him.

"When I was a boy, I wished my mother would come for me one day." He found a shell on the ground and tossed it in the water. "When my dad married, I thought I'd have a mother." Leo rubbed the back of his neck. "The first Mother's Day, I picked flowers out of the garden in our house." He gave her a shaky smile. "She threw them in the trash and told me she wasn't my mother."

Tali gasped.

"She said I was the son of a piece of trash who sold me to my father and left me." He saw tears in Tali's eyes, but Leo didn't want pity, especially from her.

"She lied. Please, let Agustina tell you the truth."

Leo stood and offered Tali his hand. "Come on, let's get going." Twenty minutes later, they were on the main road, going downhill toward the village. Leo parked the scooter in front of *Trattoria Luciano,* an orange brick building with a large red-and-yellow sign over the door. The scent of coffee and sweet bread permeated the establishment.

Trattoria Luciano was pure Italy with its tables covered in red gingham tablecloths and a collection of antique odds and ends. Home-cooked basic Italian food. At first, Tali's presence had caused commotion among the locals. They'd stared at the woman with the shocking hair and hippy clothes. She soon won them over with her bright smile and hilarious attempts to make herself understood. She'd ordered enough food to feed an army. Soon they had a table full of donuts with vanilla ice cream, chocolate-covered croissants, cannoli, strawberry jam tart, and cappuccino.

"People are taking bets." He relaxed back on his chair. "They're waiting to see if you eat it all. I'd join in on the bets, but that wouldn't be fair as I already know your stomach is a bottomless pit."

She scrunched a paper napkin and threw it at his face. Leo ducked and laughed.

"Fine. In that case, I want you to translate for me." She stood and tapped her fork against the side of her cup.

"What are you doing?" This wouldn't end well for him, but he was having fun. Months had passed since he'd had any fun.

She ignored him. "Hi, my name is Tali. I understand that you're all taking bets on me." She looked at Leo, encouraging him to translate. "I want in. If I can't finish everything I ordered"—she pointed at the food on the table—"my friend here will pay for your meals." That was easy. She ate like a Tasmanian devil, no loss for him. "But if I eat everything, we'll leave a thirty percent tip to the waitstaff. They work hard and they deserve it."

The crowd agreed—poor suckers—and Tali finished every morsel. People took photos and videos with their mobile phones. Some would no doubt be posted to social media, and someone was bound to recognize him. Vincenzo Romano would be livid, not to mention Mariano and their father. Leo smiled, knowing that none of them would think this was funny. He was tired of allowing Vincenzo Romano to manipulate his life. Leo was a man who lived by his own rules since he was a teenager. He never gave a damn what anyone thought about his life choices. But for the past year he'd been accountable to his brother, his father, a fiancée he did not love, and her insufferable father. He'd had enough! If there were pictures and videos posted to social media, so be it. What did he care if people thought he was sleeping with Talisman? That was better than to have the truth come out, the real reason why she'd shoved, and crammed, and injected herself into his life—Agustina.

The staff took selfies with Tali and thanked her for her generosity. He had to take her away before they crowned her queen for the day. He paid the bill, grabbed Tali by her arm, and they left the *trattoria*.

Back on the Vespa, he drove to a spot near the top of the hill with a fantastic bird's-eye view of the village and public beach. When she pressed herself against his back, his body hardened. There was clearly a magnetic pull between them.

He parked on the hilltop and they dismounted. A low rock wall lined the road. They sat facing the ocean, shaded by the canopy of a towering oak tree. The morning was clear, allowing them to see the way down the hill toward the marina and the public beach. The village had been built on the side of the mountain, with the main road zigzagging along.

"This place makes me think of Positano or Portofino." She stared at the beach scene below. The beads on her face twinkled as bits of sunlight snuck through the foliage. "If I had my phone, I'd take lots of pictures."

"It might resemble those places, but we don't have their hotels, overpriced knickknacks, or the desire to attract large crowds." And they never would, if he had anything to say about it.

A wrinkle creased her forehead. "No hotels? Where do people stay when they spend the night?"

"Most people come by ferry for the day. Others spend the night in their yachts or in somebody's house if they know anyone who lives here."

A strand of hair covered one of her eyes. Without thinking, Leo moved it out of the way. "Isola Rosalia is a fishing village and will stay that way. The tourism industry here is tiny. People come for privacy, rest, and relaxation."

"I pray you're right. It would be terrible to sacrifice this paradise at the feet of the gods of greed."

"Let's go. I want to show you the outdoor market." Leo helped Tali get back on her feet. He pulled her against his chest and kissed her. Entangling her hair between his fingers, he tasted her lips. She held him as if she depended on him to keep her on her feet. He dropped a trail of tiny kisses from her mouth to her ear. "My sexy *arcobaleno.*" The world faded around them. His skin tingled and burned where she touched him. The magic broke when a red VW Beetle drove by them, stopping long enough for the driver to yell something in Italian and laugh loudly before driving off. Leo pulled away from Tali.

"What did he say?" Her face was flushed, her lips swollen.

"He offered us the use of his car for a fee." She blushed, and his heart beat a lot faster. He had to stop doing that. "Let's do some shopping."

They strolled the market, browsing the clothing and jewelry kiosks. Leo offered to buy some things for her, but she refused. Unwilling to have a scene in public, Leo kept walking.

Other market sections carried the familiar scents of fresh fruit and vegetables. Villagers stopped to chat for a minute or two. The pressure of the wedding was gone, and he enjoyed being home again.

"Do you have a boat down there?" Tali pointed to the little marina near the public beach.

"I've got a boat there, yes."

"Only one? I imagined a man like you would have an entire fleet." Her face was so severe that Leo laughed.

"I've got a yacht, kayaks, wave runners, and other boats. If I kept them all here, there'd be no room for the villagers' boats."

"Why don't you build a larger marina? It's your island." She nibbled her lower lip. Did she have any clue how cute she looked when she did that?

"It isn't necessary. Time to go home. I've kept the phone silent, but I've no doubt half the world has been calling." Leo gave Tali her helmet, before slipping his own helmet over his head. After seeing her secured on the back of his Vespa, he drove them home.

Tali rolled her mat and stowed it inside her bag. Doing yoga on this private, pristine beach was dreamy. The hot sand burned her feet, so she spread her towel and sat. She'd had a fantastic time with Leo this morning. Was that a date? It couldn't be. They weren't even friends. Leo hadn't mentioned his fiancée again since they'd arrived at Isola Rosalia. Were they together again? He might have intended to keep Tali on the island until he got married, then return her to New York. She knew her chances of convincing him to talk to Agustina were, at best, fifty-fifty, no matter what he promised her. Who was this Gianna he was willing to marry, even if they were not in love? And why was he willing to marry her?

A lightbulb went off in Tali's head. Could it be Gia Romano? *The* Gia Romano, celebrity, influencer, sometimes model, and one of the most photographed and well-known women on the planet? Of course. For whom else would a man like Leonardo Guerranti give up his freedom? Tali laughed aloud. And she'd thought he might have really been attracted to her. What an idiot. Why would any man have a chicken leg when he had filet mignon available at any time? That settled it. Her virginity was relatively safe. She might as well walk around naked as a jaybird, because Leo was playing her for a fool. His kisses and sexy talk were all an act to keep her happy on this island. At least until he resolved whatever business problems Tali had created for him with her marriage story. That thought should make her happy, shouldn't it? She wouldn't have to betray her parents. But the knot in her stomach didn't mean happiness. She dropped her shoulders. Tears burned behind her eyes, and Tali was glad to be alone. She rubbed her eyes, wiping any evidence off her cheeks.

This morning, when they came back from the village, Leo had given her back her phone and credit cards. He kept her passport. Baby steps, she told herself. He'd placed an app blocking her from accessing most social media websites. She didn't like how he'd invaded her privacy by installing an app on her phone, but she chose to pick her battles.

In the evening, Tali found herself dining alone. Leo didn't give further explanation for his absence. After supper, Tali called Agustina, who was frantic after not hearing from her for a month. Tali and Leo's fake marriage scandal had headlined the financial news and gossip sites. It took much reassurance from Tali to calm her friend. By the end of the conversation, Agustina accepted that Tali was better off hiding at Isola Rosalia until the scandal died. She believed her son to be a good man who was protecting her from media attacks rather than keeping Tali as a well-tended hostage. *A mother always chooses to believe the best of her child.*

It was late when Tali got off the phone. She went out to the balcony and leaned over the railing. The conversation with Agustina left her unsettled. She didn't tell her friend that the biggest reason for her wanting to stay there was Leo. She wanted him. Sleeping with him meant breaking her own heart, and she'd be just another body who passed through his bed. He wasn't the right man for her.

She changed into a pair of denim shorts and a strapless top. The silence in the house made the sucking sound of her flip-flopssound louder than she'd prefer. Tali crossed the garden, making a beeline for the beach. She opened the blue wooden gate and stepped onto the cool sand.

"What the hell are you doing out here?" Leo's deep voice thundered behind her. A shriek escaped Tali's throat. "Stop screaming, or you'll wake up the whole house."

She stopped to catch her breath. "What do you expect when you sneak up on a person in the middle of the night? I was fixin' to go for a walk. Why are you creeping up on me like that?"

"I saw you from my office, sneaking out of the house." He stood at arm's length, his hands on his hips, legs wide apart.

"I was running away from home in flip-flops, without luggage or money." That man could make a preacher cuss. "I can't sleep and thought a stroll on the beach might help." There was zero chance of that now. "Why were you in your office at this time of night?"

"I had a video meeting with a client who lives on the other side of the world. Under different circumstances, I would have traveled to him." He narrowed his eyes.

"Circumstances can change if you talk to your momma and send me home." She kicked off her flip-flops and dug her toes in the sand. The faint sounds of seagulls squawking in the distance and the waves whooshing nearby did the trick and she started to relax.

"Let's take the stroll." He walked to the shore. Tali snorted but she followed him. "Why aren't you sleeping?"

Tali's gut told her to keep her cards close to her chest. "I called some of my friends."

"And by *friends* you mean my mother." His tone was dry and sarcastic.

"Yes." Tali looked ahead.

"What did you tell her?" He stood in front of her. "If you lie to me, you'll learn the true extent of my wrath."

"Oh, please. You don't scare me." She refused to show him intimidation.

"Talisman."

"Are you fixin' to pitch another hissy fit?" Tali made a tsking sound with her tongue as she shook her head. "I told her I'm fine, and you're protecting me from the doggone media, sheesh!"

"And she took you at your word, huh?" He looked unconvinced.

"I'm not a liar." She moved past him and kept walking. "I reassured her I'm fine, and as soon as this situation is over, you'll send me home in one piece." She'd told him a partial truth. What kept him here? Surely it couldn't be her, not when he had more than enough people to watch her. The house was a beautiful fortress. "Was the house already here when you purchased the land?"

He stopped and stared at the mansion, half-hidden in the dark. "No, I had it built to my specifications." Leo lay down on the sand, patting the spot next to him. "It's built to provide the best views while keeping away prying eyes."

Tali rolled her eyes, but she sat by him anyway. What if she ignored her reason for coming here? What if she overlooked that Leo was a ruthless billionaire who didn't care about other people's feelings? He protected his brother, his father, and his former fiancée. If only she had someone like him in her life. Someone who looked out for her and protected her. Not that she needed to be protected, she wasn't a child. But it had to be nice to know that you could depend on someone to be there and have your back.

Leonardo Guerranti wasn't a man to aim for someone as low as her. Their differences were more significant than social and monetary. He'd never choose a woman like her. He preferred women from his own social circle. Wealthy women with the best education and connections. She had nothing, and she came from nothing. No, that was not true. Her parents loved her. But this meant nothing in Leo's world.

"Will you answer a question for me?" She spoke as she stared at the stars. This was a view you didn't get when you lived in a big city. "Why did you build such a big house if you want to be alone?"

"Because it makes me happy."

She detected a note of annoyance in his voice.

"Now it's your turn to answer my question. Do you only do the things you think make other people happy?" He leaned back, his elbows digging in the sand.

"Doing things for other people makes me happy." He had touched a sore subject. People accused her of hiding her true self. Ridiculous. Helping others *was* her true self.

"You're a hypocrite."

Tali fought to stop herself from slapping him.

"You want to hit me, to yell at me to shut up. That's natural." He tossed a shell into the ocean. "But you swallow your feelings. You think you're a better person than me."

She tried to stand in a huff. "Why are you dumping this on me right now? We were having a good time, and then you chose to insult me."

He pulled her back. "No, I want you to admit something about yourself." He wrapped a warm, strong hand around her upper arm.

"What? Stop speaking in riddles!" She flashed indignant eyes at him.

"You're a passionate woman. Beneath that good girl act, you're more fire than ice."

She clenched her jaw.

"You want to save the world because you think you know better than everyone else." He pulled her closer. "People like me, we're polluters, we're wasteful. Why should I build this huge house for myself?" He mocked her. "You sit on your high moral throne. You'd rather have your hippy clothes than expensive, wasteful haute couture. In the meantime, you couldn't wait for me to return your mobile phone. You flew on a jet from New York to London to continue your stalking campaign but criticized me for having my own plane."

He was right. Maybe Tali was a hypocrite, but she didn't know how to be anything else. Tali blinked, unable to stem the flow of tears. Leo put an arm around her shoulders.

"I-I'm so sorry." She pulled away, but he embraced her in what she could only explain as a gentle hug. The sort of hug an adult gives to a child who didn't feel well.

"Why are you sorry?"

"I can't afford to cry." She wiped the last tears from her cheeks.

"Why not?" he whispered. "You're human."

"I was one month shy of eighteen when my parents died. A drunk driver hit the car head-on." She wiped her face again with her hands. "Crying and grieving were drowning me, and I swallowed my emotions for survival. I moved to New York and created a life for myself. I can't afford weakness."

What did Leo know about loss? About surviving by the skin of your teeth? He'd been born at the top of the mountain. He'd never scratched the bottom of the barrel. He gave orders and people complied. He never had to hustle to keep a job or put up with impossible bosses who thought he was easy prey. He was the last man in the world from whom she expected sympathy. Yet here they were, on a beach, with his arm wrapped around her. She leaned her head on his shoulder and Leo rocked her the way one does to soothe a child. She should push him away, but the fantasy would vanish with the light if she waited.

CHAPTER SIX

Seagulls squawking nearby woke Leo. He sat up on the cool sand. The ocean whooshed and sparkled with not even a sailboat on the horizon. Early sunrise had brought hues of gold, orange, and greens to the island. Tali slept soundly beside him, her head resting on her arm. She'd cried last night, and he'd wanted to protect her from whatever made her so miserable. His instinct pushed him to shelter her. He'd kept her away from his brother and father, just as he had in New York when he called the police and told them it was all a mistake and she didn't really break into his office. He didn't understand the impulse pushing him to do that. Perhaps this mess would never have happened if he'd pressed the charges against her. This woman had been a stranger to him until she broke into his office. Who was she to make him feel these things?

Last night he'd held her in his arms. Their connection pleased him, perhaps too much. With all his heart, he wished to tell her everything would be fine, but he didn't. Leo wasn't going to speak to Agustina, ever. He'd keep Tali with him until the bank merger was complete. Then he'd send her back to New York. By then, her reputation would be in tatters. The world would know she was a liar and a stalker. If Agustina tried to sell the story of his birth, her association with Tali would mean that nobody would touch it. They'd all be afraid of him and what he'd do if they messed with him again. But what about Tali? Here at Isola Rosalia, she was under his protection. She had no idea that every paparazzi and rubbish reporter was looking for her. But the moment he sent her back to New York, she'd have to fight the barbarians alone. He could stop right now, before it was too late.

Leo rubbed a hand over his face. Sentimentality was a weakness, and he didn't invest feelings in any woman. Gianna was the one exception to this rule because Leo had known her from when she was a shy little girl in need of a friend. He enjoyed sex, but he never offered love or commitment. Leo peeked at Tali, who'd mumbled something in her sleep. Why did he worry? Talisman was here for one reason...money. She'd take whatever he gave her, but she wouldn't invest her heart. She disapproved of him, and she'd made her opinions clear from the start.

How had she survived on her own in New York City? An eighteen-year-old young woman living alone faced dangers anywhere. She told him she swallowed her emotions to survive, but how did she survive? Did teenage Tali con rich men willing to hand a pretty girl whatever she requested in exchange for sex? New York was expensive. Did she make enough money as a yoga teacher to afford an apartment and all the expenses?

A knot formed in Leo's stomach, so tight and painful he bit his lower lip to stop a grunt. Bile rose to his throat. No! His Tali wouldn't sell herself to any man. She might have conned a few. Hell, she was working a con on him now. She'd had the nerve to tell the world they were married. But that was a far cry from prostitution. He shook his head. It didn't matter what she did or didn't do. He'd send her away soon.

If he was alone, he'd get naked and go for a swim. But Tali lay next to him. If he removed his clothes, it wouldn't be for swimming. Leo raised himself to his full height and stretched his aching muscles. Tali was still asleep. Rather than wake her, he picked her up in his arms and walked home. He placed her on her bed and, agonizingly, pulled himself away and left the room. She was a woman like any other woman. He didn't care about her or how difficult of a life she had. A lack of sex had caused this obsession with her. Leo retired to his office. Pouring a double whiskey, he plopped down on a chair behind his new desk.

He was jealous. His guts twisted again. This gut-wrenching resentment was unacceptable. He was guided by his brain, never his libido or his heart.

Leo opened his laptop and scrolled through dozens of emails until he found the one with Tali's background report. Tali told him her parents had died in a car accident. She left out that she was in the car too and she'd almost died. She'd needed months of therapy before she could walk again. Her parents had left her a tiny house with a hefty mortgage. After selling her home and repaying the bank, she had enough money for a one-way plane ticket to New York and a short stay in a motel. She'd found a job as a yoga instructor in a posh gym during the day and became a part-time server at night. She took on private clients and stopped waitressing when the yoga business took off the ground.

The woman described in the report and the woman who broke into his offices twice and told the world she was his wife didn't seem to be the same person. By sleeping with her, Leo would kill two birds with one stone. He'd prove her a cold-hearted conniving woman and get this sexual frustration out of his system. A knock on the door pulled him out of his introspection.

"Come in!"

Talisman strode into his office wearing a tight-fitting knitted striped dress in every color of the rainbow. He'd been right when he'd picked it out from the back of the shop. The dress emphasized every delicious curve of her hot body. Hands on her hips, she stared him down.

"Where are my clothes?" She was back to her usual bossy

self. He found it easier to deal with this Talisman than the soft woman who'd cried on his shoulder last night. "What the heck is happening here?" Tali did a complete 180 and, with her mouth wide open, she examined the room.

"You're wearing them." Tali's breasts were a magnet for Leo's eyes, so round and luscious.

She pursed her lips and shot him an exaggerated eye roll. "You know this dress is *not* mine. And there were bags full of clothes in my room." She went back to studying his office. "This room. Holy guacamole."

"I went back to the market in the afternoon and bought you some clothes." She looked ready to defy him, so he spoke fast. "You didn't bring enough things to stay here for more than three days." Tali turned around to examine the large oil painting of a double orange begonia. "What's wrong with the room?"

"Well, nothing, that's what's shocking." She smiled, and her dimples threatened to charm his pants off his body. "You have bright orange chairs, a blue couch, a modern desk, and colorful art. Did your designer make a huge mistake?"

"You don't like it?"

She stayed silent.

He didn't care about her opinion, of course. But why was she so quiet? Talisman always had something to say. "Well?"

"I love it!" She leaned on his desk and her face glowed. "I've never been in this room before. I was expecting more clear plastic furniture and plain white walls. Who did this?"

"Me. I designed it." He pushed his chair back. "But I may not keep it. You're right. It is too much."

"No!" She opened her aquamarine eyes until he thought they'd pop out of her face. "Don't you dare! This room is beautiful and bright and I love it! Fire your fancy decorator and re-do this entire house. In fact—" She stopped, a touch of drama on her face.

"In fact, what?"

"I can help you." She crossed her arms, jutting out her chin.

"I appreciate your offer, but you won't be staying long enough to follow through on it." He regretted the comment as soon as it came out of his mouth. Her face fell and the smile disappeared.

"You're right. I forgot." She veered toward the door. "Thank you for the clothes."

Leo had an idea. Maybe not a brilliant one, but why the hell not? "Stay a moment, please." He went ahead, using caution. "I had one of my boats converted to all-electric, with solar power. They delivered it a couple of days ago and I must evaluate it." This was a task he had to do anyway. Why not have her tag along? She'd be a lot more fun than one of his guards.

Tali faced him with a raised eyebrow, pursed lips, and shoulders pushed back. He'd hurt her feelings, and now she had a bit of an attitude.

"Come with me." He really hoped she would say yes, which was puzzling. Leo pushed aside that thought. "*Per favore*?"

"When do we leave?"

"In one hour. Don't eat breakfast or you might get seasick." That was easier than he'd expected. "We'll have lunch later. Oh, and Tali?"

"What?"

"Never wear a bra. I love your breasts." Tali's cheeks took on the color of a plum as she rushed out of the office. All her talk of soulmates and saving the planet was garbage. She wanted him as much as he wanted her.

As Leo sailed the boat away from the marina, Tali kept her eyes on the little village perched on the hillsides. She stood at the stern of the boat, wearing the red bikini she'd found in the bags of clothes Leo had bought for her. He refused to tell her where they were going, making the trip into a mysterious game. The coast appeared as a faint line on the horizon, the boat making a slow turn to the left. They sailed parallel to the island, headed to the side owned by Leo. A boat indeed, Tali scoffed. They were sailing on a small luxury yacht—the kind that tourists rented for a day or two when they were on vacation. The boat had a cabin with a bed and a bathroom. Not that she went snooping around in there, but Leo had made a point of letting her know.

Leonardo steered the boat from the helm with the confidence of a man used to this sort of thing. His white cotton shirt flapped in the breeze. He'd rolled the sleeves to his elbows. The back of the leather seat hid the rest of him from Tali's view. He turned his head back. Dark sunglasses hid his eyes. She dropped onto one of the soft, luxurious vinyl seats in the customized open deck, not risking a fall while the boat sailed at high speed. Leo laughed and turned his attention forward again. She didn't trust her sea legs. The breeze played with her long hair, which Tali had forgotten to braid before leaving the house.

She didn't like the helplessness of her situation. It wasn't the yacht or not knowing where Leo was taking her—it was everything. Leonardo didn't trust her. She'd done her best to prove herself to him. Like a sheep, Tali did everything she was told. She wanted to go home, but where was her home? She lived alone in a tiny, overpriced studio apartment. She spent her time volunteering for different charities and working hard to make ends meet. That life had been satisfactory but dull. After the car accident, dull Appealed to her. She chose to keep people at bay. That was preferable to taking the risk of losing the people she loved. Agustina managed to get through her wall of protection. To repay her kindness, Tali toed her way out of the boundaries she'd set for herself.

Leo steered the boat closer to the island, pointing out his house and his strip of beach. He'd built the house on a peninsula. Three sides faced the ocean. Earlier she'd offered to help him decorate. That was an impulse, but she'd meant it. Tali cared more for that house than for her place in New York. He'd hurt her feelings by reminding her she wouldn't have enough time to redecorate. Why had that upset her? That wasn't news to her, for goodness sake. They sailed past the house into an unfamiliar part of the island.

Leo slowed the boat. They approached a series of white rock formations tall as walls. Leo stopped, letting the boat bob on the water. He plopped next to Tali.

"Are you all right?" He removed his sunglasses.

"I'm fine. It's my first time on a boat and—" Tali stopped to catch her breath.

"Are you seasick?" Was that concern she heard in his voice?

"I was going to say it's exhilarating." She moved a strand of hair away from her face.

"Wait for the best part. See the arch in the rocks?" He pointed toward a large arc shape not far ahead. "There's a hidden spot that's perfect for swimming and snorkeling."

"I don't know how to snorkel." Warning bells went off in Tali's head. As if in some movie, she heard a voice in her head repeating *danger, danger*. He must have read the fear in her eyes because he caressed her cheek.

"I'll teach you everything you need to know." He sailed through the natural arch formation. They dropped anchor and Leo disappeared below deck, returning with snorkeling gear. "I'm a certified Scuba Diver. You'll be safe with me."

Leo's patience made the lessons easy. He kept them within the shallow areas and pointed out colorful marine life. They swam into beautiful caves, where the water made the walls appear blue, but he didn't take her any deeper than three or four feet. After a while, he led her to a narrow band of sand. The sun shone brightly from the middle of the sky. Without another human in sight, they could have been the last two people left on Earth. On the sand bar, Leo lay back, closing his eyes, and Tali braided her wet hair. Remorse engulfed her. Living a life of leisure, like some upper-crust, jet-setting girl, went against her moral compass.

Come on. She was lying to herself. That wasn't her moral compass consuming her from the inside. She loved spending time with Leo, enjoying his attention and charisma. The chemistry they shared ought to terrify her, but he thrilled her. She'd never have gone snorkeling with someone else. After the'car accident, she made risk-free choices. Everything she'd done since they met went against her better judgment. She went to Europe by herself. She was staying with him on an island where she knew no one. He offered to take her snorkeling, and she trusted him and enjoyed herself.

"Aren't you going to ask me about the scar on my back?" She seldom thought about it because she'd had few opportunities to show anyone her back. But she'd been wearing a bikini, so he must have noticed.

"No, not unless you want to talk about it." His voice held a note of sympathy, but not enough to be called pity.

She wanted to get this out of the way, so like peeling off a bandage, she blurted out, "It's from a surgery I needed after the car accident. I'm okay now, so I don't want your pity."

"How did you enjoy your first snorkeling experience, *arcobaleno?*" Leo stretched his long, tanned legs.

Maybe she didn't want pity, but at least a word of acknowledgment would've been nice. "Fascinating." She squeezed the water out of her hair . "I'd expect to find this place jam-packed by crowds."

"I own this place, and I've made deals with the Italian government to keep it pristine. I allow marine biologists and other scientists to use it for studies and investigations to help sea life, but no tourists." He lay back and closed his eyes. "By the way, the scar is not a big deal. Don't let it bother you."

Did he really think the scar wasn't a big deal? Or was it one of those things people said to be nice? Leo nice? She almost laughed at that thought. Anyway, was Leo a conservationist? Did she misjudge him? "What are those words on your chest?" She'd been curious about his tattoos for a long time.

He 'umped to his feet. "Time to return to the boat. I'm hungry."

She grabbed his ankle. "Is it about a woman? Did she break your little black heart?"

He snapped a stiff look in her direction. "No, Ms. Nosey. They're the symbols of the St. Marco Regiment. The words mean *by sea, by land*. And that's the end of the question-and-answer period." He swam to the boat and Tali followed, climbing aboard after him.

Leo disappeared inside the cabin. Tali opened the large tote bag she'd brought with her, grateful that she'd remembered to bring a towel. She dried herself and shimmied into the sundress she'd worn that morning. The boat bobbed gently on the water. Tali sat on the soft vinyl seat and looked around. She closed her eyes and let the sound of water lapping against the boat wind her down.

"What's wrong? You're not having a good time?" Leo was back on deck. The sun was behind him, giving him a golden aura.

"I'm fine. Aren't you going to get dressed?" Now that they were back on the boat, it was next to impossible to keep her eyes off his body.

"I'm wearing swimming trunks. We're on a boat." He looked at her as if she'd grown a second head. "You're the one overdressed. Where's the bikini? Did it shrink?" He opened a bottle of water, drinking half of the content in one gulp.

"Are you saying you think I'm fat?" Who the hell did he think he was, making judgments about her body? "I'm about fixin' to dump this tea all over your head!"

"You sure can be touchy!" He laughed at her. "You're not fat, you're perfect. That's the problem."

"Problem? There's no problem here." Where was he going with this line of conversation?

"Not for you, for me." He finished his water and tossed the bottle in the cooler.

"Plastic bottles? Honestly, do you give a damn about the planet? Like…at all?" She bit her bottom lip. Dang. That judgmental attitude was showing again.

"Forgive me. I'm not as enlightened about these issues as you." He said the right words, but Tali's blood boiled at the sarcasm dripping from his voice. When he sat next to her, Tali leaned away. She deserved his mockery. It wasn't the first time she'd accused him of such things.

"You're so annoying! You were saying you have a problem?" Might as well find out what he meant.

"My problem is I want to rip off your clothes and have sex with you until we're exhausted, then wait half an hour and do it again."

Tali dropped her lower jaw. What if he did just that? A little shiver ran down her spine. Now she understood the reason for her sudden lousy mood. He hadn't touched her all morning. No, that wasn't true either. He'd touched her in the ways necessary to teach her to snorkel and to show her around the caverns. Not the way he'd handled her before…and she resented it. Good grief. He traced a line below her chin and stopped between her breasts. Tali's nipples hardened.

"I have erotic dreams about you every night." He whispered the words. "Look what you do to me." He placed her hand on his crotch. She gripped the thick length. He took her hand and slipped it under his swimming trunks. She caressed the tip with her fingers. "Stroke me."

She rubbed him with firm, slow motions, taking her cues from his reactions. He threw back his head and closed his eyes. His chest rose and fell. Tali enjoyed every bit of control she had over him at that moment.

He covered her fingers with one hand. "Stop." He pulled himself away.

Tali searched his face. "Did I do something wrong?" She was having difficulty getting air into her lungs.

"Of course not. But there's a better place and time for this, my sexy *arcobaleno*." He squeezed her nipples. "Let's eat our food, because I know you're starving." He winked and walked away.

Tali closed her eyes. She was here to convince him to talk to Agustina, but she was a selfish coward. And a hypocrite too. She allowed him to use her for his enjoyment, and she loved it. Her parents' faces filled her mind. *Momma and daddy, I'm so sorry for disappointing you.*

Leo returned with a basket full of cheeses, olives, fresh bread, and chicken salad. He laid it all on the table in front of them. Tali's mouth watered. She wasn't betraying any ideals by eating this food.

She finished her last bite and took the bull by the horn. "What's happening with your brother's business deal? It's time to fulfill your promise to talk to Agustina."

He put the tableware back in the basket but stopped long enough to frown at her. "Your little stunt at the trattoria added fuel to the fire."

"How?" Good grief, what had she done now?

"People took videos and photos of us, and we were on the Internet before we got home." His mouth tightened.

He couldn't be serious. "No! You said the people here are on your side." Would she ever stop making mistakes long enough to get out of her own way? She only posted photos online to advertise her yoga classes. Who would take her seriously now, after the craziness of the past month?

"There were tourists there. I don't control what people do with their social media accounts." He bared his teeth. "And I don't want to discuss Agustina. Are you so scared of your feelings you'd rather ruin a fun day?"

"I don't know what you're talking about."

He was close enough that she saw the depth of his gray-blue irises. She smelled the salt on his skin. "You're such a liar!" He tilted her face and sank his tongue into her welcoming mouth as he pushed her against the leather seat. He sparked an inner fire in her belly. Then Leo pulled away, using the gentlest movements. She read his eyes, and what she saw there scared her. Pure, raw emotions. A reflection of herself. Recognition. "You're mine. But you're such a little liar. What will I do with you?"

His bittersweet words stung deep in Tali's heart. Leo returned to the helm of the boat. Time to go home. Her vision blurred. Two large tears ran down her scorching cheeks. The boat picked up speed and the wind blew her tears away. They'd had a good time, and that's all he ought to know. She'd cried enough in front of him already.

The return trip was faster, but didn't it always feel that way? They spoke only when necessary. A strange silence permeated the atmosphere. What should she expect from him now?

Once home, Leo excused himself to shower and work. Regardless of what he'd said earlier, he'd chosen not to have sex with her. He didn't have supper with her either, locking himself in his office instead. She must have bored him to pieces. Of course she wasn't at the level of the alluring and refined Gianna. Tali slumped deeper into her pillows and closed her eyes. Obviously he was avoiding her.

She was a stupid idiot. Leo was a womanizer, and she

wasn't *special.* As soon as these screwball circumstances were over, he'd send her home with a broken heart. Tali flipped to one side and pulled the covers to her chin.

She was wasting away her life, afraid of living it to the fullest. Always fearful of everything, especially change. In her mind, she was still the teenage girl lost in the world without her parents. Tali punched the pillow. She'd spent her childhood overprotected by her mother and lacking a father figure for months. She was twenty-six years old. She should not be upset because an arrogant schmuck didn't consider her worthy of being another forgettable name in his lengthy list of lovers.

Chapter Seven

Leo closed his laptop and flicked the switch of his desk lamp to illuminate the office. Today had not gone the way he'd planned. He'd lost himself in Tali's adventurous spirit. They connected in a way that went beyond the physical aspect. She enjoyed learning to snorkel and exploring the caves as much as he did. She didn't care that her hair got wet or that the sun might leave tan lines on her skin. He'd never had so much harmless fun with a woman in his life. Leo lived by a code. He refused to become sentimentally attached to any woman. Falling in love was not worth the risk of pain. But Tali was off-beat and a far cry from the sophisticated women he took to his bed.

There were always women in his life, of course. Although not as many as the media portrayed. Most of them were clients that he accompanied to particular events. Many didn't want to look as though they were being followed by security everywhere and asked Leo to act as their date. Celebrities were the most common. Who wanted to be photographed on a red carpet with a bodyguard?

Leo's real lovers were discreet, experienced women who knew their relationships had expiration dates. He demanded zero drama. He offered them great sex, expensive gifts, vacations, etc., until he got bored with them.

A month ago, he'd told himself that Tali was an insult to good taste. In truth, her peculiar beauty aroused and startled him. He wanted to be wrong about Tali. Why the hell did he want that? Big deal if she was innocent. She meant nothing to him, less than nothing. He was *not* falling for her.

He wasn't like his father. Fausto Guerranti was a weak man who allowed women to walk all over him. Leo watched the women in his father's life cheat on him, use him for his money, and treat him like a bank account. Love turned men weak and stupid.

Tali's game was to reconcile Leo with his mother. Agustina must have promised her a hefty sum if she managed to obtain her objective. Then there was the business of the media scandal. Those online rags paid good money for salacious stories, and information was money. If he sent her away now, she'd go straight to them again and sell any of the juicy details of his life. Why had he not thought of this angle before he brought her to his home? Well, that was a stupid question. He knew exactly why. He'd refused to think about it because he wanted to sleep with her and was willing to take any risk. But here they were, a month later, and he'd barely touched her. He spent day and night fantasizing about her. The nights were the worst. She invaded his dreams when he managed to get some sleep and awoke frustrated.

Leo tapped his fingers on his desktop. He enjoyed spending time with her. He liked the way she giggled at his jokes. She entertained him with her stories about growing up in the American South and all her funny little comments, many of which she had to explain to him. God help him, he reveled in sparring with her. That colorful, exotic bird fascinated, exasperated, and kept him in an eternal state of sexual arousal. Having sex with her would get her out of his system. She wanted him too. It was time to taste the forbidden fruit. With a purposeful stride, he left his office and ran upstairs.

Leo knocked on the heavy oak door. A moment later, Tali opened it wearing a short white satin robe with tiny red roses. With a clean face and a simple ponytail, she looked nothing like the sexy lovers who waited for him at the end of a hard day. She looked innocent, stunning, and the sexiest woman he'd ever seen.

He entered the room, closed the door, and caressed her velvet-soft cheek. She shivered and leaned against his hand. He lowered his head, enjoying the fusion of Jasmine and vanilla he'd associate with her for the rest of his life, a sweet, gentle scent that soothed his restless spirit. He dropped soft kisses on her neck until he found the erratic beat of her pulse. He suckled on that pulse until she melted against him.

He peeled away his shirt. Tali brushed her fingers over his tattoos, patting every ridge and depression on his chest. When she opened her mouth, he grazed his lips against hers. He nibbled on her lower lip. She was soft and pliable, like warm honey. Why had he waited so long to do this? He entered her mouth with his tongue. A surge of blood rushed to his shaft. With his large, strong hands, he felt his way down her back, over the silky robe. She was so pretty, so beautiful and sweet. She belonged right here, with him. Grabbing her bottom with both hands, he pulled her against him. Leo was losing control. Her lovely round cheeks had a deep pink hue.

"Leo, we need to talk."

"Not tonight. Unless you want me to leave. Is that it?" He held her at arm's length.

"No. Please, don't go." The urgency in her voice pleased him to his core. Yes, she wanted him. "But there's something that you need to know, and I want to say it." He covered her mouth with one hand.

"Whatever it is, tell me later." She lowered her eyes to his chest and nodded. Leo sighed with relief.

Shutting down the warning bells in his head, Leo pulled the fabric belt that cinched Tali's waist and tossed it on the floor. He tugged at her robe, uncovering her shoulders. She was naked under that thin piece of silk. Had she been waiting for him? He pulled the robe until it fell around their feet. She was soft and warm. Her plump breasts jiggled. He cupped them with his hands. He had the very irrational sensation that she belonged to him now. An awareness, a gut reaction that they'd been doing this act forever. How could that be? No, it was the moment. He was putting too much meaning into something as ordinary as sex. If that was so, why did it feel that whatever was happening between them was anything but ordinary? Not just now, but since the moment they'd laid eyes on each other for the first time.

"Kneel and pull down my shorts." He kept his voice controlled by sheer strength of willpower.

Tali dropped to her knees. His erection sprang in front of her as his shorts fell around his feet. He placed his hands on each side of her face and made her look up. He'd dreamed of this moment for so long. She was on her knees in front of him, which was the most erotic thing he'd ever experienced.

"Stroke me."

She caressed his thighs and held his penis with trembling hands. She examined him as if she'd never seen a naked man before. She rubbed the tip and smiled when he jerked and expanded in her hands. A ragged sigh left his lungs as Leo shuddered.

"Take me in your mouth, Talisman." He strained to hold on to some semblance of control. She enveloped his swollen member with her mouth and fingers, guiding the speed of her movements by keeping his hands on both sides of her head. She used her tongue to tease him. She wrapped her other arm around him and took hold of his butt, pulling him forward. Her movement almost pushed Leo over the edge. He gasped and shivered. One more minute and he'd explode. Leo gritted his teeth and growled as he pulled himself out of Tali's mouth.

"Did I do something wrong?" Tali had remained on her knees, but he pulled her up, crushed her against his chest.

"No, my sweetheart. This would've been over too soon if we didn't stop." He fought to catch his breath.

"Oh," she whispered against his chest.

"And there's a lot more that I want to do with you tonight." He'd waited too long. He'd fantasized about her for an eternity. One night wasn't enough, but it was a start. He was glad now that nothing had happened on the boat. Perhaps another day, but not the first time. He let his hands roam over her soft curves. She was his Aphrodite, his goddess of love and the sea. What a fool he'd been to stay away from her for so long.

"What do you want to do?" She blushed again, the prettiest shade of pink he'd ever seen on a woman. She was gorgeous. "I mean, besides the usual. I mean, do you have something specific in mind?" She tripped over her words.

Leo smiled. "Climb on the bed and lie on your back. Where do you keep your underwear?" She pointed at the dressing room door. "Stay here." He rummaged through the drawers until he found what he wanted. Her eyes were closed when he returned. "I'm going to tie you up."

Tali's eyes flew open, revealing fear and excitement. She extended both arms behind her head.

"Yes, that's perfect." He used two pairs of panties to tie Tali's hands to the headboard. She wiggled. "Are you okay?" He wanted to control her body, but he would never hurt her.

"Yes. It's just that, well, I've never done this before." The silky smoothness of her voice rattled every fiber of his being.

He looked into her eyes. "I will never hurt you. Do you trust me?" She nodded her head. "I need you to say the words. Do you trust me?"

"Yes, I trust you." Her voice wobbled. Her eyes were glassy. Yes, she was ready.

"If at any point you want me to stop, tell me." She nodded. He straddled her, taking her breasts in his hands. They spilled through his fingers. He suckled on one nipple and she convulsed beneath him. Her body was ever so sensitive to his touch.

He kissed, licked, and explored every inch of her face and breasts. He found the spots that made her convulse and beg for more. He ravaged her swollen lips.

He pulled his head away a couple of inches to look at her face. She whispered to him, imploring him to take her. She rubbed herself against him. Leo roared. Who was controlling who?

"No, my *arcobaleno*, not yet. I'm going to devour you first." She buckled and yanked her arms so hard he thought she might rip the panties he'd used to tie her. He slid down her body. She lifted her smooth legs, rested them on his shoulders. He brushed his thumb over her nerve center. Tali spasmed and screamed something unintelligible. Her legs wobbled, but she kept them wide apart. "Tell me what you like." The blush on her cheeks had spread to her breasts.

"I don't know." She gasped for air. "I've never done this before."

Leo frowned. "You don't know?"

She shook her head from side to side.

How was that possible? "Has nobody ever given you oral sex?"

"No. Don't…don't stop, please!" She struggled to speak.

If that was true, he would be the first man to taste her. The first man to touch her this way. How had she reached the age of twenty-six years without doing this? The idea of Tali with another lover was a sucker punch to Leo's solar plexus. He put the thought out of his mind, afraid jealousy might consume him.

He opened her pink slit, revealing her moist center and distended clitoris. She gasped and made all sorts of little noises that caused his shaft to grow painfully hard. He sucked the swollen gem as she bucked and screamed, reaching peak after peak. He penetrated her with his tongue while his fingers kept a torturous rotation on her clitoris. His erection threatened to burst. This satisfaction and pleasure went beyond anything he'd experienced before. He pulled her torso up from the bed, opening her, and making her vulnerable in every way. He entered her again with one finger. Not deep, only enough to keep her begging for more. Then he rubbed her juices on his erection. He moved up on her body, taking his engorged penis with one hand and rubbing it against her swollen nub. She was amazing. So responsive, so sweet. This most intimate caress shattered something fragile inside him, something he'd never felt before tonight. He was on the edge of coming home.

He could enter her now, she was ready for him. Or he could keep torturing them both. Her hot skin dripped with sweat. Her breasts jiggled as she moved from side to side. This glorious sex goddess was his woman. With the last strength he could muster, Leo pulled himself away and climbed out of bed. "I'm getting a condom." He answered the question in her eyes. She nodded.

Leo rolled the condom over his stiff shaft with shaky hands and climbed back on top of Tali. They were face to face now. She wrapped her legs around his waist again. He claimed her mouth as if they had been doing this act for ages. "Are you ready?" She nodded, but there was cloudiness in her eyes. Could it be fear? No, she did not fear him. "Are you sure you want to keep going?" She nodded again, and this time she whispered a soft, "Yes."

Leo positioned his shaft at her entrance, releasing control. He pounded into Tali, penetrating her with abandon. Leo almost didn't feel the rupture of flesh, but he did feel it, shocking him into stillness. She was a virgin, and he'd taken her with brute force. "Tali?" But how was it possible she was a virgin? Yes, he'd wished, fantasized, dreamed about the possibility, but he'd never expected it.

She opened her eyes. A pained expression on her beautiful face was followed by the intense force of desire. Her legs tightened around him. "I'm okay. Please...don't stop." She writhed beneath him.

Leo dropped a tender kiss on Tali's soft lips. This wasn't the time for questions. They were here, where he'd wanted to have her for so long. He pulled himself out. She needed time to get used to him inside her. She opened her lips, but he placed a finger over her mouth. He entered her again, this time with gentle strength. He repeated the movement several times until she met each thrust with one of her own. "Yes, that's it. We have all the time in the world." She moved her hips, those hips that drove him to distraction. He untied her hands. Her eyes shone like stars. She burrowed her fingers in his hair and pulled a long strand, giggling when he yelped. He deserved the payback.

Their bodies entwined, moved to the same rhythm—a new yet familiar sensation, as if they'd done this thing many times, for ages. They kissed again, a mind-numbing, consuming, endless kiss. She was slick and pure fire. He sank into her time and again. Each penetration threatened to send him over the edge. In the recesses of his mind, he heard her scream his name. She arched her body, shuddering and squirming. He drove her to climatic, earth-shattering moments time and time again. She was a delicious, ripe fruit, and he enjoyed her every minute. Every nerve in Leo's body was electrified. A jolt of pleasure shot from his brutally aching arousal. He held Tali's hips, driving himself inside her, throbbing and tingling. Leo's climax overtook him in a series of shattering spasms. He called out her name until he collapsed on her warm body.

Leo lay back on his side of the bed. Damn him...and damn her too. Now he knew she'd never had another lover. His head was full of questions, and his body would demand more satisfaction soon. He couldn't stay, because he'd take her again and again, like some madman. He was shocked and confused and had to sort out these new facts as soon as possible.

He jumped out of bed. "I have to go now. We'll talk about this in the morning." He disposed of the condom in the bathroom and left Tali's room without looking back. If he looked back, he wouldn't leave at all. Out in the hall, it occurred to him Tali hadn't said a word, nothing. What was going on in her head? He'd stay and talk to her if he was a good man. But he wasn't an honorable man. He just couldn't do it. After one last look at the closed door, Leo walked away.

Tali flipped over onto her stomach. What had she done? She hid her face in her arm and sobbed. Was what they did so meaningless to Leonardo that he left without...Well, without what exactly? Was she hoping to sleep in his arms the rest of the night? No, that only happened in romance novels. This was real life. She meant nothing to him...less than nothing. But shouldn't there be some conversation? Some polite words? She was acting stupid. The images of what they'd done wrestled in her mind. Not one of the sexual encounter stories she heard from other girls compared to what Leo did to her. She'd allowed him to take control of her as no other person ever had. She grimaced at the sight of the panties he'd used to tie her up. They'd been discarded on the floor, the same way he'd dumped her when he was done.

Tali sat up, pulling her legs against her chest. She wiped the tears with a pillowcase. They'd never removed the bedspread. She slumped her shoulders forward and rested her head on her knees, wrapping both arms around her legs. The deed was done. She'd chosen Leonardo Guerranti as her first lover, and what a lover he was. She could not complain about his sexual expertise. But she hadn't been enough for him. She knew she wouldn't be enough for a man with his experience. There were moments during their lovemaking she thought perhaps she measured up to his other women. But as soon as they finished, he couldn't wait to get away from her.

Tears welled up in her eyes again. Tali wiped them away with the back of her hands. She was *not* going to cry again over Leo. There'd be time to lick her wounds when she was away from here, away from his domain. This was the time to put on her big girl panties and act like an adult. Her chest tightened and burned from the pressure not to cry. She'd given him her body…she refused to hand him her mental well-being. Tali scoffed. Maybe he expected her to fly off the handle and run after him. To cry and beg for an explanation? She scoffed again. He thought the sun came up whenever he opened his eyes.

She deserved an explanation. Good manners demanded you say something nice after a person had sex with you. Tali nibbled her bottom lip until she tasted blood. She'd rather be hung by her fingernails, tarred and feathered rather than ask him for an explanation. She sure wished she could go to the kitchen for tea. But if he saw her, he'd think she was looking for him. Mister High-and-Mighty wouldn't believe all she wanted was a cup of sweet tea.

She jumped off the bed. Her body ached in places she didn't remember using. She put her clothes away and filled the tub. Finding one of her old T-shirts in a drawer, she placed it near the tub along with a towel. The last thing she wanted to do right now was wear any clothes Leo had bought for her. She soaked in hot water, wishing the water had magical powers to erase all traces of Leo from her body. She hadn't made a mistake. Having a real relationship with Leonardo was never a possibility. She reached for the shampoo and massaged it into her scalp. But she expected more than the *I have to go now. We'll talk about this in the morning* comment he'd thrown at her without any care whatsoever. It was a long time before she drained the tub and finished conditioning and rinsing her hair under the shower.

Walking barefoot into her bedroom, she eyed her phone, tempting her from where she'd left it charging on a nightstand. What if she called Agustina, told her the plan didn't work, and asked her for help getting back home? Agustina had grown up in Ponza. She must know someone willing to take her to the mainland. Getting to the airport in Rome and buying a ticket to New York might take a couple of days, but it could be done. Damn it, he still had her passport and driver's license. She'd forgotten that she gave them to him when she decided to come with him to Italy. It made going through customs faster. Everything was faster and more efficient when it involved Leonardo Guerranti. Later she was too busy thinking about having sex with the man to remember to ask him to return her documents. He'd never talk to Agustina. He was playing with her, and she let him because she wanted to sleep with him. Now she'd slept with him, and he'd proven that she meant nothing to him once and for all. Not that he needed to prove it, that was a given. In the morning she'd demand that he send her back to New York.

What about her reason for seeking him out in the first place? Her goal, from the beginning, was to find a way for Agustina to have a heart-to-heart conversation with her son and tell him the truth. Leonardo had spent his life knowing one side of the story, probably a lie. Agustina had placed all her motherly hopes on Tali to create a bridge with her son. Tali had faced worse monsters than this stuck-up rich Italian. She'd faced a horrible car accident, the loss of her parents, and the loss of her entire life. She wasn't giving up on helping her friend, even if all she achieved was one conversation between a son and a mother who loved him very much. She wasn't in love with Leonardo, she wasn't! He was hateful, mean-spirited, and nothing like her soulmate. She'd never fallen in love before, and she was *not* falling in love now. Tali towel-dried her hair and crawled into bed. Sleep didn't come easy, but it was dreamless and restful when it did because her mind was made up. She would never have sex with Leonardo again.

Chapter Eight

Wild strands of ebony hair unraveled across Leo's forehead. He plowed a hand through it, then propelled himself forward at jogging speed. An early morning beach run always helped him clear his head. Discovering Tali's virginity had confused and alarmed him. She'd always made her desire for him self-evident. He hadn't worked hard to convince her to sleep with him. Why did she wait so long to have sex, then choose a man with whom she didn't have a chance in hell for a relationship? Blood rushed to Leo's face as he recalled his wish for her innocence. What did she expect from him now? He'd been exponentially honest with her from the beginning. They were never going to have a relationship.

Her frenzied responses gave him pleasure such as he'd never experienced. She held nothing back when she gave herself to him. She showed genuine responses, but her reasons were deceptive. They had to be. Leo reached a standstill and pulled back his shoulders to stretch his aching muscles.

He found pleasure in being her first lover. He wasn't a chauvinist and wouldn't have thought less of her if she'd been with other men before him. But jealousy left him wanting to punch any rival in the throat. Leo had never known jealousy in his entire life, not even when his younger brother was born. He'd focused on making himself worthy of his last name.

He was the son of a greedy maid who abandoned him when he was born. He'd been luckier than most people to be accepted by one of the wealthiest families in Italy, despite being illegitimate. As long as he proved himself honorable and respectable and made his family proud, he had no reason to be jealous of anyone. He'd honored his family name in the military, receiving medals of valor for his work in undercover operations. He'd gone on to open his own business and make it fabulously successful. He'd repaid his grandparents and his father's generosity many times over. Jealousy wasn't part of his life until now.

Tali responded to him in a way no other woman before her had. She gave herself without reservations. Her responses were genuine, but her reasons weren't. The seed of an idea germinated in his brain. He threw his head back and laughed. A dry, humorless noise. Just as his mother sold him at birth, Talisman sold her virginity—a trap to guilt him into meeting with Agustina. Leo crackled every knuckle on his hands with precision.

When all else fails, work on a man's guilt. How much money had his mother offered her to get the job done? She hadn't waited so many years to sell her virginity for a pittance. He'd met self-serving moneygrubbers, but none were as persistent as Talisman. A pulse on the side of his neck beat at a furious rate. She'd sold her innocence to the wrong devil. He'd allow no escape or have any mercy for her now. A vengeful, twisted smirk crossed his face. The conning little witch underestimated him, which became Tali's Achilles' heel. Leo jogged back home.

He was working in his office when there was a knock at the door. He looked at the clock on the computer screen. Lunchtime. Did Tali sleep all morning? He closed his laptop computer. "Come in!"

Tali opened the door and strolled inside. Her damned mix of Jasmine and vanilla scents filled the room.

"Morning!" Her smile was big and bright. She obviously thought her plan had worked. "I stopped by the kitchen for a cup of sweet tea, but the place is empty." Her red sleeveless sundress showed him an ample view of her chest, then floated past her hips and ankles. Did she look different this morning? No, he was imagining things.

"I gave the staff the weekend off." A shuttered expression moved over Tali's exquisite face. "You'll have to make the tea yourself, I'm afraid." He checked his phone, and there was yet another text from Mariano. When they were giving away patience, his brother had been the last one in line.

"I don't mind." She shrugged her shoulders. "But it's bizarre for you to do that while we're still here."

"You aren't here on vacation, and I'm not bound to provide you with luxury accommodations." A deep shade of pink crawled up her face. How did a woman without principles manage such perfect blushes? She retreated toward the door. "Come back and sit with me, Talisman." She ignored his order and kept walking. Leo jumped to his feet and blocked her path.

She raised an eyebrow at him. "I don't know what bee got under your bonnet, but I refuse to stay and take your attitude." With both hands on her hips, she looked like a tiny fighter ready to go on the defense.

"You are going to do whatever the hell I say. Now sit down!" He snarled his order.

Tali's back stiffened, but she stood her ground.

"I suppose when you know you made a terrible mistake, your reaction is to run, like most cowards."

She glared as he boasted. "I've never cowered from any*one* or any*thing*. What's your problem? After last night I thought our…relationship…was at least amicable."

Her Southern accent was more pronounced when her temper flared. Leo lowered his eyes to her sparkling pink lips.

"I demand that you return my documents. I want to go back to New York."

"Tell me, how much money did Agustina pay you to sell

your virginity?" He scrutinized her face for any signs of shame.

She shook her head, a symbol of denial but not guilt or embarrassment. "Sell my…what are you talking about?" One of her hands flew to her chest. She appeared the precise image of unworldliness and honesty. She'd be nominated for an Oscar for this performance if this was a movie.

He repeated his question, this time using deliberate, slow timing. "How much money did Agustina pay you to give your virginity to me?" Tali's hand flew across his cheek and she slapped him—not once but twice.

"I'm not a prostitute!" She took three steps backward. "How dare you speak like that to me!"

Leo's ear was ringing from her slaps. Tali's soft cry broke through the silence. The sensation of a knife plunging into his chest stopped the insult that was ready to fly out of his mouth. Hers was a gentle sobbing, not the over-the-top dramatic weeping he'd prepared himself to watch.

Rubbing his cheek, Leo backed away. Tali had slumped into the sofa and held her head in her hands. Her sobs made him want to embrace her, apologize, and ask what he could do to fix the situation. He didn't know what to do, and this angered him.

"Don't turn me into the villain in this story." Leo forced his hands into the pockets of his jeans. "Your greed put you in this situation." It irked him how he yearned to hold her in his arms and reassure her everything would be fine. She raised herself from the sofa and wiped her face with her hands. "You lied to me, at least by omission." His resolve for vengeance dissipated, and he held out a box of tissues, but she ignored the gesture.

"I told you I was a virgin last night. I did." Her eyes were flat and cloudy, and the corners of her mouth curled into a frown. It dawned on Leo this was the first time he'd seen such a sad appearance on Tali's face.

"You did no such thing," he hollered back at her. "If you wanted me to know you were a virgin, you had plenty of opportunities. No! I do not believe you!"

She grabbed the box of tissues he still stupidly held in his hand and threw it against the wall. "I told you that I'd never done it before."

She had. *Dio Mio*, she did say words to that effect when he asked if she was comfortable being tied up. Was it possible he'd misunderstood? No, this was another lie. She'd never said she was a virgin. His heart pounded inside his chest. Was she speaking the truth?

"You're lying again," he grunted back. "I asked you if you were okay getting tied up, and you said you'd never done it before, but you agreed to do it anyway."

"In that case, we're at an impasse. What are you going to do with me now?" The question was like an arrow shot straight into his heart.

Leo turned away from the haunted look in her eyes. He believed her. She was a proven liar, and he never forgave a lie. Everything in his life experience taught him to never trust a liar. But a voice deep in his subconscious told him this was the truth. Against all odds, he believed her…and she trusted him. Every crazy thing that happened from the moment they met should tell him she was untrustworthy. Yet here they were again. He believed her, and she trusted him. She gave herself to him last night, trusting him with her life, knowing he'd never hurt her. He desired to carry her to the nearest bed and make love until they were too exhausted to think.

Mariano texted him again. Soft footsteps broke through the fog in his brain, and the door made a dull sound when she left. He had to settle things with Mariano, because Leo would not, *could* not, marry Gianna. Not now. Not after what had happened between Tali and himself last night. He grabbed the phone and dialed his brother's number.

Tali dropped the doorknob. Her heart hammered at the rhythm of a drumbeat inside her chest. She dragged herself to the kitchen. Good ole Southern comfort food was what she needed. Macaroni and cheese, fried chicken—the stuff her momma cooked for her when she had a bad day. Mamma always said that nothing in the world could be so terrible that some of her food and a lot of love couldn't fix. She opened the refrigerators. This hoity-toity kitchen had nothing resembling her momma's cooking. Tiny beads of sweat dripped from her forehead. Tali wiped them off with her fingers. How could Leo dare accuse her of selling herself? Why had she given herself to that beast of a man? He was a disgusting pig, no offense to the pigs. She checked every cabinet in the kitchen, banging each door. Stupid, dull white kitchen. She had to escape this damned house.

Tali flung open the back door and sprinted through the garden. The house suffocated her. Even the beautiful garden where she'd spent so much time confined her. During their first lunch here, Leo had told her that some prisons didn't look like prisons, but they still held people captive or words to that effect. She hadn't believed him. How could it be possible for someone to be captive in Heaven? How wrong she was. How quickly had Heaven become Hell for her. She had no escape from his terrible accusation.

Tali screamed when Leo grabbed her arm and spun her like a ballet dancer. They faced each other like two gladiators in Rome's Colosseum. She twisted her hands into fists to punch his chest. Leo seized her wrists. He rotated her arms until they were behind her.

"*Già abbastanza*!" He pulled her against himself. "Enough already. I don't want to hurt you."

"Too late for that." What did a little physical pain mean now after he'd broken her heart? She breathed in his woody, earthy scent. The effort of unshed tears scorched the inside of her poor, swollen eyelids. She refused to cry in front of him. This worthless man didn't deserve her tears. She bowed her head. If he saw her eyes, he'd read in them the pain he'd caused her, the pain strangling her at this moment. Her legs wobbled as if they were made of gelatin. If she managed to escape him, where would she go? Was there a place where she'd be able to hide from herself? She was a fool. Her cheeks burned thinking about what they'd done last night. The things she let him do. The stuff she *begged* him to do. The things she gladly did to him at his command. No, there was no escaping from any of it. Not even if the Earth swallowed her would she escape her utter humiliation.

She shifted, still fighting to slip out of his constraint. Leo grunted like a wounded animal. He eased the pressure of his hands on her wrists. His chin rested on the top of her head. He wasn't letting her go. By what right was he doing this to her? Zero. He had no right to her, not anymore.

"Where were you going, *arcobaleno?*" His voice was thick. Was he sorry for what he'd said to her? Of course not. She pressed her lips together. "Tali?"

"Away from you." *Don't cry. Just don't cry. He'll let you go as soon as he's sure you won't keep running. You cry and he wins.* She despised the unfamiliar numbed sound of her voice. How much more pathetic could she be?

"That's not going to happen, *arcobaleno.*" They looked into each other's eyes again. "At least not until I say so."

"Bless your shriveled, tiny, black heart."

His sensual mouth quivered, then broke into a full laugh.

Her heart sank into her stomach. How gorgeous he looked when he laughed. And how stupid she was for wanting more. She'd become masochistic since meeting him. The minute he turned on the charm, she ignored the horrible things he did and said to her. She was the dumbest woman on this side of the Mississippi…or whatever big river ran down the whole of Italy.

"I want to hear the truth. Why did you hide your virginity from me?" He fixed his metal-gray eyes on her. Now he wanted to know. What difference would it make? He'd made up his mind about her long ago without giving her a snowball's chance in hell to show him she meant no harm. She knew it, but she still offered herself to him on a silver platter.

"Why are you asking me? I told you the truth, but you didn't believe me." She chewed her bottom lip.

"You blamed me, and we both know you were lying. Tell me the truth."

He dropped her arms and Tali massaged her wrists. They didn't hurt, and he didn't hold her tight. Not after the first couple of seconds, when he stopped her assault on him. She'd never hit a person in her life. She should apologize.

"Stop calling me a liar, you beast. Why should I waste my time? You won't believe me anyway." She put her pride aside for a moment, just a moment. "I'm sorry for hitting you."

He shrugged it off. "It happens, and I deserved it. Now answer my questiolyn, *per favore*."

Tali gave an almost imperceptible nod. Why had she never noticed how quick he forgave all the little things? Maybe he was so focused on the big things that he dismissed anything he considered minor. Perhaps he didn't forgive so much as he ignored anything that got in his way. "I planned to tell you." When he raised an eyebrow, Tali rushed her explanation. "I swear it, at least at first. I wanted to sleep with you. But I had this life plan, and you weren't in it." He'd laugh if she explained it to him. Everyone did, so she'd learned to keep her plans to herself. She knew to keep everything to herself.

"What life plan?" He pulled her toward the koi pond, where they had their first lunch together. Today they sat on the little stone wall surrounding part of the pond.

"I decided years ago that I would only have sex with my soulmate." Tali dipped her fingers in the cool water. "No offense, but that's not you." She made ripples in the water to avoid his piercing, intelligent, steely eyes.

"Yes, I know. That perfect man who doesn't pollute but works to save the planet, doesn't drink from plastic bottles, etc."

She flashed him a cautioning glare.

"Okay, I'll stop teasing you. Go on."

"My plans flew out the window when we met in New York."

Leo nodded. There was a sort of understanding on his face. Was she right when she'd thought she saw a flash of recognition on his face the first time they met? She thought she'd seen it, but then so many things had happened that she'd convinced herself it was all in her imagination. "And then everything got all muddled up. You're my friend's son. We'll never see each other again. I decided not to sleep with you." She feigned interest in the colorful fish. "But then you brought me to this island."

"And you changed your mind again." He finished her thought. "That still doesn't explain why you didn't tell me."

"I'm getting there, geez." The man's patience was smaller than a mosquito. "I was afraid if I told you what I was, that I'd never been with a man, you wouldn't sleep with me." Tali's throat was as dry as the Sahara Desert. "I didn't want you to reject me."

"Why would I reject you? What kind of man do you think I am?" The arrogant note in his voice forced Tali to turn her head. Had he really just asked that question?

"The kind who doesn't want an inexperienced woman in bed." Tali grimaced. "The kind who already thought the worst of me."

"I wouldn't reject you over inexperience, *arcobaleno*. But I'd have considered that you waited a long time to have a lover, and I'm not the one who will give you a happily ever after." A somber expression came over his face.

"And there it is." She pointed her index finger at him.

"What?" He was looking at her as though she'd grown a second head.

"Regret. You regret sleeping with me." She closed her eyes and refused to watch a hint of dissatisfaction or remorse on his face.

"Open your eyes, *arcobaleno,* and listen to me." He placed his hands on each side of her face. "I will never regret being your first lover, ever."

"You won't?" She searched his eyes for a hint of mockery but found none.

"Tali, I brought you here because I wanted us to be lovers come hell or high water." He smiled, and he appeared to be ten years younger. Tali knitted her eyebrows together. It dawned on her that he looked his actual age when he smiled. He was only thirty-five years old. He was not an old man, but beneath his barely civilized appearance was a man who seemed jaded by life. However, the times she'd seen him laugh or give a real smile, she had a glimpse of a different sort of man behind the façade.

"Now it's my time to confess." He fiddled with the collar of his shirt, opening the three top buttons as if they were choking him. "I'm glad to be the only man to have touched you like that." He cleared his throat, and Tali frowned. "I'm not a chauvinist, I swear it. But there's something about you. I don't know what it is, something that pulls me to you. I'm selfish, but I don't look at your virginity as some trophy. I just wanted you to be mine, only mine." He stopped talking and raked his fingers through his hair.

That was one of his little tells when he was uncomfortable.

Tali recognized it now.

But he didn't stay quiet for long. "Quit frowning, and let's go to the village to eat." He stood and extended a hand in her direction.

"Why do you assume I want to eat now?" She accepted his hand.

"I also assume Christmas is in December. I saw the remnants of your travels through the kitchen. Some doors came off their hinges. If I don't feed you, I won't have a house left by this afternoon." He offered her a crooked, funny smile. Her heart melted into a puddle.

"Sorry about that. I couldn't find the ingredients to make macaroni and cheese." She giggled when he raised an eyebrow.

"I'll add them to the very top of the grocery list." Hand in hand, they walked to the garage where he kept his collection of motorcycles and scooters. Tali crossed her leg over the back of Leo's favorite Vespa. His admission shocked her. That was the one thing she'd never expected to hear from him. A tiny flame of hope lit her heart.

Chapter Nine

Sitting in his Rome office, Leonardo closed his laptop and stretched back on his chair. Tali wasn't the person who sold the fake story of their wedding to the media. The culprit was the security guard he'd met the first time he'd visited his new London office. The man was a new hire who hadn't been adequately vetted. After feeling the pressure and receiving warnings from Leo's legal team, the man had confessed. He'd sold the story to a gossip website, and their photographers had shown up in record time. Everybody had accused Tali, including the website. That made the story easier to believe. That wasn't to say she was blameless in the incident. Had she not followed him to London and lied about being his wife, none of this would have happened.

After a week of traveling between London and Rome, Leo had now implemented a series of changes to the hiring process for his company and the bank. This problem could never happen again. He should talk to Tali and let her know her intuition was correct. After all, Tali had first suggested the guard could be guilty, but Leo had been hell-bent on blaming her. However, if he was honest with her, she would expect him to keep his word and call Agustina, which he would never do. He had to neutralize his mother's threat before sending Tali back to New York.

Leonardo's desk phone beeped twice. His assistant. "*Si*?"

"*Signor* Guerranti, *Signorina* Romano is here."

He hadn't seen Gianna since the meeting in Mariano's office. It was time they had a private conversation. "Have her come in."

The tall, coltish young woman strolled into his office like a model on a catwalk. She stopped to look at a Picasso hanging on the wall. Gianna was well put together as always, in wide-legged khaki pants and a white crocheted tank top. Couture houses begged her to wear their clothes. She was everything he'd thought he'd wanted in a woman until a different sort of woman crashed into his life in a rainbow of colors and hippy clothes.

"Gianna!" He grinned and gave her a heartfelt hug. The young woman, as usual, was the picture of quiet composure which at times could appear aloof. His brother accused her of being arrogant and distant.

"Leo!" A wide smile brightened her face. "I never understood why you have this strange painting in your office. You despise Cubism."

"That was a gift from a client. I'm not here often. Better here than at home." They paused for a moment then laughed.

"I think it's time we talk the way we did before my *Papà* suggested marriage." She wrapped her hand around his forearm. "Take me to that new *gelateria* by the Colosseum."

The way he remembered things, her father hadn't *suggested* anything. His demands were extortion. Leo kept his opinion to himself because he didn't want to start their conversation with an argument. "You'll have to show me. I haven't been there in ages." He grabbed his black leather jacket from the back of his chair.

The trendy ice cream parlor contained an outdoor sitting area. Although it was teeming with customers, the hostess found a table for them, with an umbrella for shade.

"You'll love this place." A waiter brought them their menus. "They make the best *gelato* in the whole of Italy."

Leonardo cast a glance around. They sat facing one of the main tourist attractions of Rome. This wouldn't have been his first choice of venue. He'd prefer to be back on the island, having *gelato* with Tali. Nevertheless, he enjoyed Gianna's company. "Is their *fregola* any good?" He scanned the menu.

"You always order *cioccolato*. I thought you didn't even like strawberries." She wiggled her eyebrows then gave him a knowing look. What was going on inside that pretty head? "Never mind. Yes, it's delicious. I'll have some too."

They had to raise their voices to order their food. The chatter of the customers was loud and constant. A woman was fruitlessly trying to calm a little girl who'd dropped her cone on the floor. Leo leaned forward, closer to Gianna. "Listen, Gia, I'm sorry for—"

Gianna raised a hand. "It's okay. *Papà* gave me a choice, and I chose you because we're friends. I'm the one who should be sorry. You didn't deserve to be put on the spot like that."

Her father had put both of them in an impossible situation. "I was willing to do it."

The corners of Gianna's lips took a slight turn upward. "I know, but not anymore…." Her voice drifted.

"No, not anymore." He looked into her light green eyes. "I just can't."

"Boy, she must be *eccezionale*." Gianna winked.

"Who must be exceptional?" This conversation wasn't going as Leo expected.

"The girl with the colorful hair. What's her name?" Gianna rested her chin on one perfectly manicured hand.

Leo didn't answer.

"Talisman, I think."

There was no point in discussing Tali with Gianna.

"You look happier. More like the young man you were when I was growing up."

"You're imagining things." He was the same man he was before he met Talisman. If anything was different, that was due to his relief about the end of their engagement.

"I'm not. You're falling for Talisman. You look...younger. Anger always made you look older than your years." The waiter brought their *gelatos*. With a child's delight, Gianna dug her spoon into her cup.

Leo tasted his strawberry *gelato*, desperate to change the conversation. "You're right. This is delicious." He looked at his cup. "I have to bring—." He stopped, but too late.

"If Talisman likes *gelato*, you must bring her here."

Leo ignored Gianna's comment. "What will your father do about the merger now that we're not getting married?" A shadow passed over Gianna's face. She concentrated on her food.

"*Papà* has some ideas, but nothing I want to discuss now." She cleared her throat. "I'll deal with it. I won't let *Papà* destroy something for which your family worked so hard."

"Not my family. The bank is Mariano's work." Gianna grimaced at the sound of that name. "Are you still afraid of him, Gia?" He used the name he'd called her when she was a kid and ran to him crying after Mariano said something mean to her.

"I'm not afraid of your brother. But he is horrible to me, always has been." She was using selective memory. Mariano wasn't always horrible to her. There was a time when he was a sweet, charming boy. He'd changed after his mother died with her lover in a car accident. They all did, in different ways.

They finished their *gelatos*, and then he dropped Gianna at her apartment.

After stopping by his father's penthouse, Leonardo hopped on his helicopter and flew home. Tali was there, waiting for him. His unsophisticated, uncultured, unable-to-keep-her-mouth-shut Tali. The last person who should occupy his mind. Leo refused to let her go—his walking disaster. Not yet. Not because he was falling for her. Gianna didn't know what she was talking about. She'd never even met Tali. But he did enjoy spending time with her. Now that they knew the truth about how the fake story got out, his family had no more reasons to pressure him to send her away. If anything, it was Mariano's fault for not having all his employees sign a confidentiality agreement.

All he wanted to do tonight was to have a lovely evening at home with Tali. He'd worked eighteen-hour days to shorten his time away from the island. He'd given the staff the day off to celebrate the Feast of San Silverio. Traditionally he attended the festival every year. He liked to spend time with the people and enjoy the festivities. But his time with Tali was running short. He'd attend next year.

Tali stepped on a partially buried shell. She screamed in pain and kicked it, blasting dry sand everywhere. Why had she looked him up? She should've known Leo wasn't living like a monk while he was away. But what really had her fit to be tied were the photos of him having a romantic lunch with his fiancée. He'd sworn it was over. But he'd lied to her again to get in her pants. She opened her heart to him, and what did he do? He'd played her for an idiot.

The thrumming of helicopter blades broke through the silence of the beach. In spite of herself, she started heading back to the house. She'd beenso sure he'd stay in Rome and spend another romantic night with his perfect fiancée. For all she knew, he wasn't working as he'd said. He was probably with Gianna the whole time he was away. Had he returned to send her packing? Good. She wanted to go home, or at least return to New York. She was clear now that she didn't have a home. She had a place to sleep and keep her things, but not a home. Home was a place with people you loved who loved you back. Home was what she had with her parents. When they died, she had nothing because she wanted nothing. She didn't want to love another person and lose them again. But now…

Tali stomped through the kitchen and the big, boring living room on her way to the stairs as Leo did the same from the opposite direction. They were on a collision course, but he extended his arms and stopped her from crashing into him.

"We have to stop meeting this way, *arcobaleno*."

She pulled away from him. "Don't touch me!" She planted both hands on her hips. How dare he touch her after spending the afternoon with another woman? And when it came to Leonardo Guerranti, spending the afternoon, meant he ended up in bed with that woman at some point. He was a filthy pig.

Leo's smile turned into a frown. "What the hell is wrong with you?"

"You wanna know what's wrong with me?" She shoved her phone in his face. "*This* is what's wrong with me. I saw the photos of you and your perfect little girlfriend at lunch this afternoon." She shoved her phone back into her pocket and headed for the stairs. "I had no idea you could be so lovey-dovey." If she looked at his face, she'd scream until the cows came home. He captured her, knocking her off balance for a second.

"Is that all, *arcobaleno*?" The beast had the indecency to laugh. "I'd didn't know you were so jealous."

He was a liar and a cheater, and she'd had enough. "I said don't touch me!" She pulled her arm, but he tightened his grasp. She wasn't jealous—she was mad as hell.

"Gianna and I aren't back together," he murmured in a husky tone. Her heart raced, but she refused to accept his answer. She wasn't an idiot, whatever he might think. "You're telling me not to believe my own eyes?" He was a real piece of work.

Leo encircled Tali's waist with both of his arms. "Absolutely. I'm telling you to believe me over anything you see on any damned phone." His words didn't sound like an order when his lust-filled eyes burned through her.

"Man, that's rich. You expect me to develop blind faith in you, but *you* don't trust *me* one tiny inch." Her words, rather than deter him, seemed to encourage him. He lowered his head and claimed her lips in a possessive caress. A pool of liquid fire melted at her core.

He carried her to his suite. Tali hadn't been back there after her first night on the island. He settled her feet on the floor and pushed her against the wall. She pulled his shirt, digging her nails into the warm skin of his back. He thrust his tongue into her mouth. She moaned, and he leaned into her. He lifted the hem of her dress and pulled on her thong.

"What are you doing?"

He rubbed the bundle of nerves at the center of her womanhood. Tali fractured into a million pieces. No, this wasn't how she'd intended things to go.

"Lower my pants…*now*." He whispered the simple command in her ear.

With trembling fingers, Tali unzipped his jeans. Digging her fingers between the fabric and his warm skin, she pulled his pants and underwear until they fell on the floor. She touched his engorged length, pleased to feel him quiver.

"You still want to know what I'm going to do?" He lifted her flat against the wall, penetrating her with one swift, mind-numbing thrust. "What I've wanted to do all day long."

Tali closed her eyes. It was useless to fight her desire. With every wild thrust, he imprinted himself in her soul. She wrapped both legs around his waist and released the last vestiges of coherent thought left in her brain. An intense jolt sparked a flame in her as wave after wave of orgasmic spasms raked her body. She loved this man. She loved him so much. Somewhere in the recesses of her mind, she heard Leo let out a raw cry of release as his climax rolled through him.

"Are you okay?" Leo whispered the words in Tali's ear. His husky voice and warm breath gave her goosebumps. She'd kept her legs wrapped around him, and he'd stayed buried inside her, owning her even after they'd finished the act.

"How could you have sex with me the same day you got back with your fianc . . . " She'd just had sex with a man engaged to marry another woman. How could she sink so deep in the mud? She loved him. The situation was crazy, incomprehensible, impossible, but she loved him. That wasn't an excuse. It was her truth.

"Damn you, I told you already. Gianna and I aren't together." Leo pushed himself away and pounded the wall with one fist.

There was a dull ache beneath her ribcage. She wanted to believe him, but the pictures didn't lie. They were together, and they'd left the restaurant together. "Liar! I saw the photos of the two of you having lunch together. I'm not stupid." She fixed her hair with shaky hands.

"You also saw photos of you and me. You read the fake news about our marriage, and was that true?" Leo let out an emotional roar.

"Of course not. But—"

"No buts. Not this time. You know I'm telling you the truth." He held her face in both hands. "I've never cheated on a woman, and I won't start now."

"Then why were you two together this afternoon?" Tali's heart birthed a spark of hope.

"I don't have to explain myself. My word must be enough for you." His face seemed sculptured out of cold marble.

"Whatever." Tali turned to dash out of the room. He wasn't going to explain himself to her. Who was she, after all? She was the woman who disrupted his life for a while. For a moment, Tali had forgotten her place on this island, in this house, in his life. Leo rammed his body against the door, blocking the exit.

"Forget it. You're not escaping again." He stood with his legs wide apart, his mane of black hair tousled and wild around his face. "My family and Gianna's family have been friends for generations. She and I have been friends since childhood."

"I don't care anymore." Tali walked to the balcony, but she didn't open the doors. She stood there, staring at the sea, working to squash the silly ray of hope that refused to die.

"After our engagement of convenience exploded in our faces, Gianna left Italy to get away from the scandal. Today she went to my office to talk." Leo stood behind her but didn't touch her.

When he spoke again, Tali felt his breath on her hair. She swallowed the dry knot in her throat.

"We cleared the air, Tali. She's not in love with me, nor am I with her. We've never had sex. We've never even kissed."

"I don't know if that makes things better or worse. You would stay faithful to a wife to whom you would never make love?"

"Yes. For as long as the marriage was supposed to last. Gianna's father is terminally ill, and he's worried his daughter might fall for someone who will use her for her money. He insists she marries now to a man he trusts to look out for her best interests."

Tali shifted position, and her heart raced when she found Leo's chiseled face merely inches away. She flashed him a look of disbelief. "Do you hear yourself?" Tali's hand flew to her forehead. "You're all demented. This is not the eighteenth century. People don't do arranged marriages anymore."

"Don't be naïve, Talisman. People make arranged marriages all the time. Power marries power, and money marries money, and that's the way the world works." With unapologetic eyes, Leo's words left no room for doubts. He believed everything he said.

She put a hand on his chest and shoved him. "That's not the way *my* world works." She wished with all her heart to take a moral high ground. But all she could think was that he wasn't together with Gianna. "This planning, plotting, and putting money above love…it's plain wrong."

He wrapped his hands over her shoulders and pulled her closer. "And who made you the authority on right and wrong?" He was still nude. She'd ripped his shirt off at some point, but she didn't remember doing that. Only the evidence on the floor told her that she had. He wasn't engaged, and he was a free man. And he was right. Who the hell was she to make pronouncements over right and wrong?

She pushed him again until they fell together on his bed—he on his back and she on top of him. When he tried to touch her, she took his arms and pulled them over his head. She should tie him up, as he'd done to her, but she didn't want to waste time looking for something she could use. Instead, she leaned close to his ear. "Take off my dress." She saw his dilated pupils. She felt the renewed hardening of his shaft against her belly. "Now!" Leo obeyed.

With the dress tossed to one side and their bodies entwined again in their mating dance, Tali rubbed herself against him. She liked having this power over him. Leo took her breasts in his hands and she lowered her torso. He took a nipple into his mouth. He nibbled on it and suckled, and then he did the same with the other. Tali sat upright and took his penis in her hand. She lifted herself and with one glorious movement she sat on him, taking all of him inside her. She was fuller than she'd ever been.

Leo grunted and bucked up on the bed, pushing deeper into her. He grabbed her from behind with both hands as Tali rode him, her breasts jiggling. Leo propped himself high enough to lick her nipples with every twitch and movement. Tali shimmied and wiggled, gasping as he moved a hand between them to rub her womanhood. He apologized for losing his last bit of control as he exploded inside her. Tali enjoyed wave after wave of his orgasm, joining him again. They climaxed together, always in tandem, with that frenzy of two people who cannot get enough of each other. When they were both spent, she dropped exhausted on his chest. Their sweat and scent mixed as their bodies recovered from their second climatic lovemaking in less than one hour.

She crawled out of bed and shimmied into her dress, unable to face him after what she'd done. She was becoming a woman she didn't recognize. Had she no dignity? No self-control? It didn't matter that she was in love with Leonardo. He didn't love her back. As if that wasn't enough, he'd admitted to her that power married power and money married money. She had neither of those things. All she had to offer him was her love, which meant nothing to a man like him. Which is why he'd never know she loved him. She'd take her secret with her and hope to get over him one day.

"Where are you going?" He sounded hoarse, even ragged.

"To my room. I need to shower."

He propped his back against the headboard. "We need to talk first."

If he wanted to tell her again there was no future for them, she didn't want to hear it. "We've talked enough for tonight, don't you think?" Her heart couldn't take more pain.

"I'm afraid we did more than that, *arcobaleno.*" His seductive lips contorted into a humorless grin. "We had unprotected sex twice, and you could be pregnant with our child."

"What?" Tali croaked the single word as she staggered to the door. He was right. "I need to be alone for a while."

"I don't think that's a good idea." The husky sound of his voice was like nails scratching a blackboard.

"Nothing that has happened since we met has been a good idea. I need a moment to myself, please." Tali spoke through clenched teeth.

Leo gazed at her with hooded eyes. "Okay, but this conversation is not over." She had no idea what he was thinking, but it couldn't be good.

Tali dragged her exhausted body to her bedroom. How did she get herself into another impossible situation? How could she be so reckless as to have unprotected sex at her age? That wasn't her fault alone. He was right there with her. Not that it mattered now. A child tied her to Leo for the rest of their lives. She dreamed of a family with a man who held her values. She and Leo might as well be from different planets. What was she going to do now? She could have an abortion. Instinct drew her hands to her belly. That might be a choice for other women, but not for her. If she had conceived a baby, she'd keep it. The child was her blood, her family, someone she could love freely and without reservations.

What if Leo didn't want to be a father? He'd do the right thing regardless of his wishes. Leo always did the right thing for his family. But if he didn't want to be a constant presence in their child's life, it would free her from him. She filled the bathtub with hot water. A bubble bath might relax her and help her with the headache threatening to erupt. She could be worried for nothing. There was a good chance she wasn't pregnant at all. This thought ought to please her, but her chest ached instead. It was a relief to lower her cold body into the hot, soapy water and close her eyes. His warning about the conversation not being over was impossible to ignore. What if he did ask her to have an abortion?

Chapter Ten

Leo downed the last of his Limoncello and put the shot glass on the white marble countertop. Looking around at the stark room, he decided it looked more like a hospital than an upscale kitchen. The room lacked color and warmth. He'd ask Tali her opinion, but he knew what she thought already. No place in this house lent itself to children. Nothing in his life lent itself to children or a wife, because he'd never wanted them. What if Tali was pregnant? A little person might be coming into this world with the right to expect his time, love, and patience. And, for goodness' sake, the child's mother. Leo grunted. The most exasperating woman he'd ever met. She was also warm and kind. She worked hard to brighten other people's days. He was sure Tali would be a loving mother.

He didn't blame her for this mess. This one was all on him. He and Mariano were the result of people who should never have had children. He'd watched his brother change after his mother started taking lovers, flaunting them like trophies, and ultimately dying with one of them. Mariano had grown into a somber, stiff-upper-lip, perfect son to their father, while Leo drowned himself in extreme sports, women, and later the military. Mariano graduated at the top of his class and followed their father's footsteps into the business world. He refused to take a step out of line. Perhaps out of fear of becoming like his mother? Unloving mothers had scarred them both. Their father was a good man, but one parent couldn't replace the other. Leo refused to put another human being through that pain.

He smelled Tali's scent before her bare feet padded into the kitchen. He'd been expecting her. That girl couldn't go long without eating. He reined in a chuckle.

"Oh, you're here." She moved past him and went straight for the refrigerator.

"Your powers of perception are amazing." He touched a button on the wall, flicking on the overhead lights. "I've already set the food on the table."

She looked adorable in her pink pajamas and long braid. Leo yearned to push her against the table and make love to her again.

The corners of her mouth lifted. "Where did you find the mac and cheese?"

He followed her to the table and they sat across from each other. "I had my father's chef make it for you. I hope you like it." Tali dipped a fork into the pot, took her first bite, and sighed.

A wave of pleasure ran down Leo's spine. "I brought it with me this afternoon."

"It's so good. Not as good as my momma's, of course. But delicious." With a serving spoon, she filled her plate with three times as much food as any woman he knew.

"I'm glad to know my father's Michelin Star chef can cook almost as well as your mother." Leo served himself some of the leftover chicken and sweet peppers he'd found in the fridge. "He also made pecan pie."

She took a drink of sweet tea before she spoke again. "How did you know I like pecan pie? And did he make the tea as well?"

"You told me your *mamma* made one every Sunday and put a slice in your lunchbox on Mondays, so you'd have something nice to start your school week." He chose not to tell her he'd made the tea while waiting for her because she'd misinterpret it and think him a sentimental idiot. He did it because he was bored and because he knew they had a tough conversation coming up.

"And you remembered?" She looked at him with a sparkle in her eyes.

Dio, there was that gushing tone in her voice.

"I'm shocked. Most of the time, you don't give a flip about what I say." And she kept eating her macaroni and cheese. Well, the gushing didn't last long, did it? Good, better that way.

They ate in silence for a while. Leo couldn't let her leave the island before finding out if she was pregnant, which meant keeping her in his home longer than he'd planned. The best-laid plans failed just as quickly as the worst plans.

After his conversation with Gianna, Leo had thought he was prepared to send Talisman home soon. Whatever happened between his brother and Gianna's father was now out of his hands. His PR department had stopped the fake news story about his marriage. As far as the world was concerned, his engagement to Gianna ended of mutual accord and they were still friends. How was he going to explain Tali's continued presence in his home? Whether or not she was pregnant was nobody else's business but theirs.

"I'm not having an abortion, just so you know." She emphasized her comment by dangerously pointing at him with her fork.

Leo coughed up the water he was drinking. "Excuse me?" What the hell was she talking about now?

Tali put down her fork and wiped her mouth with her napkin. "You're quiet, but I see the wheels turning. I decided I'm not having an abortion if I'm pregnant." She glared at him. "You can't force me to get rid of my child."

"You are, by far, the craziest woman I've ever met." He picked up the knife he'd dropped on the floor when he choked on his water.

"I knew it." Talisman jumped off her chair and took three steps back. She pointed her index finger at him as she flashed him an accusatory look. "You want me to get rid of my baby so you can go on with your life as if this never happened. Forget it."

This was not a good start for a conversation he'd never planned to have with anyone. "First of all, cut out the hysterics. You're making assumptions without asking me any questions." He pushed his plate away, forcing himself to stay calm. "We don't even know yet if you're pregnant." She opened her mouth, but he held up a hand and kept talking. "And if you are pregnant, I would never ask you to have an abortion. Indeed, I never wanted to be a father, but I'm prepared to face my responsibilities." That didn't sound warm and fuzzy. Nevertheless, it was the way he felt.

"How sweet."

Sarcasm again. She could give a master class in mockery.

"Did you hear that, baby?" She looked at her flat stomach. "Your daddy's ready to face his responsibilities. How many other kids do you have around?"

"Really? Is this how you want to play this game?" He crossed his arms and fixed disinterested eyes on her. "I don't have any children. And the odds that you're pregnant aren't great. But if you think this baby will be your golden egg, you're mistaken. I'll take care of the child if there is a child, but I won't hand you a blank check. I don't care if you're my child's mother."

Tali's hand flew across the air and slammed into his cheek. She had the right to do it, even if it wasn't politically correct. His well-thought-out words were a slap on her face first. He squashed the sting of regret burning in his chest. This conversation wasn't going as he'd planned, either. Then again, when it came to Tali, nothing ever went the way he envisioned. He'd prepared himself to have a calm and rational talk with her. He planned to reassure her that he'd support whatever she chose to do. His gut twisted and ached to think of Tali not wanting to carry their baby. If she was pregnant, he wanted that child. He'd take care of Tali as well. That was what he'd wanted to say until she flipped the script on him. Now he found himself voicing things he'd never intended or even considered.

Her accusations wounded him, brought back the pain and drama of his unwanted conception. Perhaps because he didn't expect that, not from her. Not from his Tali. He'd taken her for granted. All the time they'd been together, he'd had the upper hand. He was callous and said things to her out of anger, things he didn't believe. Now she'd turned the tables, and he'd reacted the way he always did—he'd punched harder.

"I will never—hear me well—*never* use my child to get money from a man, especially if that man is *you*."

She spat out the word *you* with so much disgust that Leo believed this to be the moment when hatred for him filled her heart.

A light flicked off in Tali's beautiful aquamarine eyes. She dashed to the door, but her step faltered. There was a thump as she hit the floor. The sounds of her gentle sobs filled the kitchen.

Leo curled his hands into fists at his sides. He had the right to be angry. Not once had she stopped to think about him, the repercussions of her actions in his life. Everything she'd done affected the lives of many people. Why did he feel like the villain in this story? Leo snorted as he threw his hands in the air. *Don't turn around. She's a drama queen. Leave.* Leo massaged the muscles on the back of his neck. He had to do something.

Tali jolted when he wrapped his arms around her shoulders and pressed her against his chest. "*Calmati, arcobaleno.* Calm down," he whispered. "I will protect you and the baby. Don't cry, *per favore*." The sensation of having held her this way for thousands of years overwhelmed Leo. What the hell was happening to him?

"How will we ever raise a happy baby together?" She drew a shaky breath.

"We'll figure it out." Leo dropped butterfly kisses on the top of Tali's head. "I promise."

She wiped her tears away. "That poor kid is fixin' to grow up all catawampus."

"I've no idea what you just said." Leo loved the strange way she expressed herself, and he loved her sense of humor. He had to send her away if she wasn't pregnant, before confusion made him do something stupid.

"I mean that any kid we raise will start deep in the hole." She pulled away from him. He didn't want to let her go, but he did. "Thank you for dinner. You can go to bed, and I'll do the dishes."

"No, listen. There's a festival this weekend in the village, our Feast of San Silverio, the patron saint of the Pontine Islands." A night without family pressures or thoughts of pregnancy would do both of them some good. Just two people having fun, like the day on the boat. "It's not as big as the one in Ponza, but it's nice. Come with me."

Tali bit her lower lip.

"Well?" He held his breath.

"Okay, sounds interesting."

Leo let out a long breath. All right, this was more like how he'd hoped the evening would go. "Wear something comfortable, because we'll be doing a lot of walking."

The smells and sounds were nothing Tali had experienced in the village during their earlier visits. According to Leo, many tourists enjoyed their festival's party atmosphere. The celebration at Isola Rosalia was less religious than the one in

Ponza. For the rest of the year, Isola Rosalia was little more than a fishing and farming village.

They parked on a side street near the harbor. Colorful banners decorated the cobblestone streets, bathed in lights from stores, restaurants, and old-fashioned streetlamps. Hand in hand, they strolled the ancient streets. Some sections of the streets were nothing more than stairs leading to corners filled with flowers and milling people. Artists sketched tourists and live music played everywhere. In Tali's eyes, the village was dressed in its finest clothes and brilliant jewels.

They walked for a long time. Everyone seemed to know Leo. They stopped to say hello, and he played with the children. She let him buy her a handmade beaded necklace from a young woman at a jewelry stand. Of course, it wasn't because she wanted a present. And she only accepted it to help the girl make a sale. Never mind that a long line of people was interested in making purchases. She was doing something good for another fellow human being. Her skin tingled when he stood behind her and closed the necklace's clasp. He brushed his fingers against her nape, and that was a most intimate caress in the middle of this crowd.

Tali cleared her throat. "Thank you, it's lovely."

"Are you hungry, *arcobaleno?*" He laughed. "Why even ask? Look, there's a vendor over there." He pulled her along, missing the *if looks could kill* glare she sent his way.

They bought two bags of *zeppole* and giant lemonades. Spotting an empty bench on another narrow street, they ran to it before another tourist could lay claim.

"Oh my gosh, these are the most amazing cream-filled donuts I've ever had!" Tali licked some of the cream stuffing off her upper lip.

"What?" Leo contorted his face into an exaggerated look of shock. "Don't ever call *zeppole* donuts!"

"But—"

"No." He put up a hand. "No buts." He pulled a *zeppole* out of his paper bag. "These little balls of deliciousness were invented in ancient Rome, and they are *not* donuts."

"Well. Lah-di-da. Pretentious donuts." She winked at him, sniffed the sweet scent and took another bite.

Tali and Leo finished their food and tossed the trash in a bin. He took her hand, and they swayed to the music from a street band. Leo led and Tali followed. She closed her eyes and imagined they were alone and in love. Her heart skipped and played along. They were happy and in love, and their world was beautiful. She let her fingers wander through his hair. The dark strands were luxurious and rebellious and beautiful, like the man himself.

"Are you having a good time, *arcobaleno*?" He whispered the words in her ear like the purr of a lion. He was sexy and masculine, and she wanted to stay in his arms forever.

"Very much." She raised her face and met the smoky expression of his approval. "You're a great dancer." He was a natural leader.

"I like who I'm holding in my arms." He lowered his head but stopped inches from her lips. The dark irises of his eyes expanded. "*Dio Mio*, you smell so damned good." The corners of his mouth lifted into a crooked little grin.

She rested her face on his chest and the world faded. There was magic in the air, and a gentle breeze swept through the place. She sent out a little heart-wish, asking that he love her because she loved him. "Oh please, you're such a liar." He was seducing her again, and she lacked the guiles to resist him.

"Don't you think you smell good?" He chuckled, and she punched his arm.

"Ouch!" He rubbed his bicep.

This was her chance to step away before she made a bigger fool of herself. "You know what I meant." She darted down the street, but he was faster.

He encircled her waist and pulled her against him.

Would he kiss her again? She hoped he would kiss her.

"Let's go down to the marina. There'll be one last firework show. Then we can go home."

Her heart plunged into her stomach. Would he ever kiss her again? After the disastrous talk about her possible pregnancy, she was sure he'd never touch her again. Then they'd danced, and that dance was so special, so beautiful. Did he not feel what she did? Did he care so little that he didn't feel the same emotions she felt? No, he did not. If he did, he'd kiss her. It was over between them. She'd better come to terms with that. Baby or no baby, Leo was done with her.

With a reluctant sigh, she let him take her through the busy street, ending at the marina. She recognized the entrance with a huge sign that read *Lungomare della Marina,* the access to the Marina Promenade. That was where Leo's electric boat had docked the day they went snorkeling in the caverns. They found a space on the ground and sat. Soon people filled the promenade. Those who arrived late watched from the street higher on the hill.

Tali glanced at Leo out of the corner of her eye. He didn't introduce her to the people who stopped to say hello. Was he embarrassed by her? She looked at her outfit. Were her tie-front top and matching pants not good enough for this celebration? Too hippy? Too loud? Gianna Romano was gorgeous and classy. Her photographs appeared on the pages of the world's best fashion magazines and social media sites. She modeled for famous fashion houses. Being seen with Tali was more than a few steps down. It was an entire flight of stairs.

Her mother's voice came through her self-deprecating thoughts. *You are perfect just the way you are, and you are beautiful and unique.* Her mother never cared what others thought of them. She was an old soul, a flower child.

"What's happening in that crazy mind?" Leo brushed his fingers over one of Tali's knees to remove some dirt. A strange yet tender act.

Tali fixed her sight on the boats bobbing in the marina. His simple act pulled at her heartstrings.

"Thinking about my momma." She cleared her throat. That was a half-truth, but at least it wasn't a lie.

"What about her?"

"I pictured her dancing in this place. She loved to dance." Memories she'd buried long ago now played like a movie in her head. "She loved music and she played it at home all the time. We danced around the house, pretending to be princesses in a big, beautiful castle. Sometimes daddy joined us when he was home." She frowned. He hadn't been home very much. Her father loved her and her momma, but that love was not enough to keep him in their home most of the time. He missed birthdays, Christmases, and school events. As a child, she never understood why he wasn't around as much as her friends' fathers. Then she told herself that she was being selfish. He was out in the world, helping people who needed him more than she did. But now the old feelings of resentment were returning, filling her heart and mind. No, she couldn't think about that. He was gone now. What was the point?

"Were they happy together, your parents?" A note of sorrow slipped into Leo's voice, but a sparkling smile brightened his face. It sparked a little too much.

"Yes. Momma told me he was her prince, the man of her dreams." But they also argued. She'd hidden in her room, but even now she could hear their raised voices. The bad memories surprised her, like one of those boxes you open and a scary clown pops out. She'd kept that box closed for a long time. "She wished me to find a man as good as my daddy." And that man wasn't Leonardo Guerranti.

"About this afternoon…." His voice trailed off.

Her heart leaped.

"Nothing happened between Gianna and me. We had a conversation, that's all."

"You don't need to explain yourself, Leo. It's none of my business." Just a conversation with his beautiful, former fiancée? Why not? What possible reason did he have to lie to her?

"You cared when I got home." He leaned back, resting his elbows on the cement.

"We owe each other nothing." She slashed herself wide open with her words. Yes, she cared. The words burned in her throat. She ached to grab him by the shoulders and shake him. How was he so blind he couldn't see how much she loved him? She watched another couple angle their heads together. The man said something, and the woman laughed a flirty little laugh. Then he kissed the tip of her nose.

"Unless you're carrying my child." His husky voice sent a shiver through her body. Carrying his child. The way he said the words scared and excited her at once. Did he hope she was pregnant? She made a tsking sound with her tongue.

Tali flipped a strand of hair that had become loose. "If I'm pregnant, I will do just fine as a single mother." What she wouldn't give for a glass of sweet tea to dampen her parched throat. "You can marry Gianna with no guilt."

Leo sat upright and held her chin in one hand.

No, she didn't mean it. Tali didn't want him to marry anyone. But why had she said that? Why did she continue to poke the bear? Reassurance. What other reason could it be? She was jealous of any female who caught his eye. She wanted him to continue reassuring her there was no other woman in his life. How utterly stupid was that?

"Gianna and I aren't back together. We're *friends.*" The intensity in his eyes confounded her. "Our friendship is worth keeping, despite the engagement debacle." Who was he trying to convince? "From the day we met in New York, I've been with no other woman but you. Nobody."

"How can you be so cavalier about marriage? Women are interchangeable for you. So much so that you replaced your momma with Mariano's mother in a heartbeat."

The blood drained from Leo's face.

That was a low blow. Yes, she knew it was a low blow. But his confession about not being with another woman since they'd met sent her brain into a tailspin. What did it mean? Or… did it mean anything at all? She was angry, and he was here, and he—

Leonardo drew a sharp breath and released her chin. Fireworks brightened the night sky, but Tali had eyes for Leo alone. He turned his face away from her, his profile like a chiseled statue. People clapped and cheered, but for Tali the sounds were white noise. As soon as the show ended, they walked back to his motorcycle in silence. He walked ahead of her with the precise march of a soldier, and this time he took the faster main road.

The next several days were filled with uncomfortable silences, broken by bits of necessary but awkward conversation, such as when Tali found a plastic bag on her bed. It was from a local pharmacy, containing several pregnancy tests Tali did her best to apologize, but Leonardo stopped her. He was not interested in her remorse. The man she'd fallen in love with during the past few months was gone. In his place was this cold, complex human being with whom Tali could not connect. When the first test turned out inconclusive, Leo left the island with the excuse that he had to get back to work. In an almost clinical tone, he informed her that he'd check in as often as possible to learn if she was pregnant. Otherwise, he'd be too occupied with business to talk to her. If she needed anything, she was to ask the staff or contact Matteo.

So that was it. He was gone, shattering her heart into

millions of pieces. How many times had she heard similar words from her father? Too many to count. She was alone in the world…again. And until she came upon her elusive soulmate, she was destined to never trust a man to stay by her side. Tali put a protective hand over her belly as she stared at the pristine waters of the Tyrrhenian Sea. What would she do if she had created a child with Leonardo Guerranti, a man who saw her and her child as nothing more than a responsibility?

Chapter Eleven

Leo released his rage and frustration by beating his punching bag into oblivion. He moved his hip, then in one swift movement he pivoted on his feet, raised his leg, and kicked the bottom section of the bag. He kept moving his body, kicking and punching with impossible accuracy. MMA fighting was part of his special training. After leaving the military, Leo continued the same grueling workout. His work demanded that he stay in the best physical shape. Beads of sweat streamed down his face, neck, and chest. He grunted each time his knuckles or his feet struck the bag. Now he was glad he'd listened to Matteo's advice to have the gym in his London penthouse remodeled while he was at Isola Rosalia. A challenging nightly workout helped him fall asleep when his head hit the pillow. Without it, he might stay up all night thinking about Tali and the baby. He'd owned this place for three years, but it had never felt like home. This was the place where he brought his lovers. More private than a hotel room. Sleeping in the same beds where he'd brought so many women had never bothered Leo… until now. For the past week, he'd slept alone in the living room. Every bedroom came with reminders that he'd rather forget. Matteo liked this place. He'd give it to his friend as a bonus for all his years of faithful work and friendship.

One week away from Tali did nothing to change Leo's disposition. Neither did the sixteen-hour workdays. But there was no escaping from his thoughts. How dare she accuse him of replacing his mother? He pounced on the bag, ignoring the pain radiating from his hands. Antonietta Baldelli had turned out to be the stepmother from Hell. When Leo was four years old, his father had married her. She'd hated him from the start, taking every opportunity to belittle him. The very idea of raising the son of a maid humiliated her, in her own words. When Mariano was born, Antonietta manufactured unfair comparisons. She joyfully reminded him that Mariano was born into a good marriage while Leo was a bastard.

His wealthy and cold-blooded grandparents demanded that Leo prove himself worthy of their family name. He tainted the family's blood, having been born to a maid of a much lower social class. A long string of nannies brought him up, and not one of them stayed long. An irritating ache spread to both of his temples. His grandparents were demanding and challenging with the staff. If they thought a nanny was soft on Leo, they fired her on the spot. Having disappointed his parents by having an affair with a servant, Fausto spent the rest of their lives trying to regain their approval. He was a kind but absentee father. It wasn't until Leo left home to join the military that Fausto worked to have a closer relationship with his firstborn son.

Leo cared about his father. When he came of age, he finally understood Fausto was a weak man. Had he ever loved Agustina? Or was she his way to rebel against his oppressive parents? Leo never asked. What would be the point? His father, a brilliant businessman, was a puppet in every other aspect of his life. He was a sad, insecure man, manipulated by his parents and the women in his life. He was a weak, pathetic excuse for a man, but he'd never turned his back on his boys. Leo had learned to accept him, with all his faults and his qualities.

The one person who loved him, and whom Leo loved from the start, was Mariano. They were as close as two brothers could be. But Mariano changed when Antonietta abandoned the family for a lover. She and the lover had died days later when their airplane crashed during a blizzard. His younger brother had closed himself off. Unlike Leo, who learned to cope with his lot through rebellion and utter disregard for his well-being, Mariano shifted his energies to his studies and work. His mild-mannered brother became an impatient perfectionist. Anyone who fell below his ridiculously high standards, such as poor little Gianna, was mocked and belittled without compassion. Leo lost his last connection to unconditional love.

He tossed the black leather gloves on the floor. If Talisman was pregnant, he'd step up. His child would never suffer the same treatment and abandonment as he had. But could he be a better father than Fausto had been to him? He could protect his child, but could he love them? Was he playing with the emotions of an innocent young woman whose real intention was to help a friend? Had Agustina concocted a sob story to convince Talisman to help her?

He walked into the shower and let the cold water cool him down. What if Tali was pregnant? She didn't fit in his life. Introducing her to the echelons of high society was the same as lighting a match in a room full of oxygen tanks. His business required him to meet with business leaders, politicians, and celebrities. People whose lives, religious beliefs, and politics were anywhere along a large spectrum. It wasn't his job to judge them, only to work with them. But Tali had a mouth that never stopped running. For someone who prided herself on being open-minded and accepting of everyone, she passed judgment on people and things she believed went against her ideals.

If she wasn't pregnant, the answer was simple—send her back to New York. She could meet that soulmate she kept talking about. Someone who'd make her happy. A man in whose life she'd fit. A man who would put her first in his life. She'd forget about him. In time, her life with him at Isola

Rosalia would be one of those memories where people choose to remember the good and forget the bad. She'd have children with that other man. She might even tell them about her adventures in the Pontine Islands. Bile rose to his throat thinking of his Tali in another man's bed. No! He had to concentrate on the present and future. Three weeks was enough time to know if she was pregnant. Leo shut off the water and wrapped a large towel around his hips. As soon as they received a negative pregnancy test, he'd put her on a plane back to New York and never give her another thought.

Tali sipped her sweet tea and breathed in the scent of the Amalfi lemon trees. The terrace was charming today, a soft ocean breeze cooling her skin. She loved a man who did not love her back. Worse yet, she might be pregnant by him. She hadn't heard from him for the past week. She hadn't even looked him up online, which was torture. How could he be so angry with her? After all his accusations, all his insults, now *he* was the injured one? Tali laughed at herself. She didn't have that kind of power over him. Yes, he was upset with her, but he wouldn't leave his home for a couple weeks over something she said.

She missed him. It took all her willpower to not call him or text him. In her head, she went over their last conversation many times. He'd been courteous, funny, even charming. Why had she accused him of exchanging his mother for another woman? She knew almost nothing of his relationship with his stepmother, but how good could it have been? The woman left her family for another man.

That didn't matter. How could Tali raise a child with Leo if he ran away whenever they fought? A happy and well-adjusted child needed parents who put them first. Did Leo plan to be present in their child's life? When the possibility of a pregnancy had first dawned on her, Tali hoped he didn't want to be involved. But after a bit of time to get used to motherhood, she had changed her mind. She wanted him fully involved. She hoped he loved their child and wanted to be a real father.

Her hopes extinguished while she waited to hear from him. A call, a text, an email…anything to tell her he was thinking about her. His silence told her what she needed to know. He didn't care. He didn't love her or their child. He promised financial assistance, and that was all he intended to offer.

She'd heard him as he'd returned home last night. The noise of the helicopter dropping him off woke her. She'd waited for him to come see her, but so far he hadn't.

Tali sniffed a fresh-baked cornetto. The Italian version of a croissant smelled delicious. Bianca prepared the breakfast table for her on the terrace, but Tali couldn't eat anything. As stupid as it was, she wanted to stay at Isola Rosalia. Her life in New York now looked pathetic and lonely. That horrible night when her parents were killed by a drunk driver came back into her mind, as unwelcome as an unexpected punch to the nose. They'd been fighting. She was in the back seat, listening to music on her phone. She hated to hear them argue. Her dad had decided to return to Africa to help an organization that was fighting the poaching of elephants. Her momma didn't want him to leave again. Tali's father was distracted. Too late, he saw the drunk driver cross the median. A head-on collision resulted. Her parents, sitting in the front seat, died instantly. Their marriage wasn't perfect, but they'd loved each other. That was why her momma always waited for him. That was why they danced and laughed and built a home together.

"I'm sorry, Momma and Daddy. You taught me to be open and to accept people as they are. To let love flow in and through me despite our differences. I used your deaths as a weapon to keep people away." What if she opened her heart to Leo and told him how she felt? An itty-bitty flame warmed her heart.

Bianca, who gave her a disapproving look when she came back and saw the food was still untouched, told her that Leo was in his office.

Now was as good a time as any. She was about to knock on the door when the noise of conversation stopped her. He wasn't alone. Another man's voice came through, loud and clear. They were arguing in Italian. Tali was learning the language, but they were speaking too fast. She didn't understand. She was turning to leave when she heard her name. Why were they talking about her? Who was this man speaking about her with such anger and disgust?

Tali rushed to the kitchen. She found Bianca and her mother preparing dinner. She pulled Biance aside and asked her if she knew who the man in the office with Leo was. Bianca didn't know. They tiptoed to Leo's office and listened at the door. Bianca's eyes widened.

"That is Signor Guerranti's brother, Signor Mariano. And he sounds *molto arriabato.*" When Tali shook her head Bianca tried to translate. "Upset. Like... angry, very angry. Signorina, we need to go."

"You go back to the kitchen, Bianca. It's okay."

Bianca seemed unsure, but Tali nodded so she walked back in the direction of the kitchen. She peeked back once, but Tali made a gesture with her hand telling her to keep going.

Tali took a deep breath. The fake marriage debacle had put Mariano's big business deal in trouble, and she should apologize to him. She inhaled a big gulp of oxygen and opened the door without knocking. Both men swiveled in her direction at the same time.

"Mariano, I assume?" She didn't want anyone to ask how she knew who he was. "I'm Talisman Broussard." Tali took firm steps toward Mariano. With a big smile, she extended her hand. Mariano raked her with his angry golden-brown eyes. Then he turned around and said something in Italian to his brother.

"Talisman! Why the hell did you come in here without knocking?" Leonardo spat the words at her.

Tali looked at Leo, and heat rose to her cheeks. He looked gorgeous in a black denim shirt. His short beard looked scruffy, as if he hadn't trimmed it in days. "I came looking for you. When I heard someone else in the office, I almost left. But I heard my name." She dropped her arm, but she wasn't ready to give up. "Mariano, I apologize for this whole mess. It wasn't my intention to cause harm to you or anybody else." Did he believe her? *Oh please, believe it,* she prayed in her heart because it was the truth.

"What is it you Americans like to say? The road to Hell is filled with good intentions?"

He stood too close for Tali's comfort, but she refused to step back. She'd apologized, but she was at the end of her rope and she refused to take any more rudeness from these men.

"Paved. It's *paved* with good intentions. And that's not an American expression. I believe it might have been French." She searched for Leo with her eyes. Any hope for his help was ruled out when the grim expression on his chiseled face deepened.

"Is this the woman that has you acting like a madman, Leonardo? Why the hell is she still here?" Mariano turned away from Tali, obviously deciding she wasn't worth his attention.

"I already told you I would send her back to New York. You and *Papà* can stop worrying, Mariano. I'm handling this problem, but I won't marry Gianna!" Leo slammed a hand on his desk. He'd continued the conversation in English. It wasn't enough to stick the knife in her chest? He had to twist it to cause the most pain?

"Why not?" He waved an arm in Tali's direction. "Don't tell me you fell in love with this person."

Talisman held her breath. Unbeknownst to him, Mariano had just asked the question Tali needed to know the most. Did Leo care for her, even a little?

"Of course not!" Leonardo articulated every word with extreme care. His voice reverberated in Tali's head. "She means nothing to me, *fratello*."

"Then why the hell have you kept her here all this time, like a princess in a tower? Protecting her from the press. From *me*, that's why." Mariano had pointed out the obvious, but he missed the more significant reason. Why did Leo keep her here? Because he wanted to take her to bed.

"I had to ensure she and Agustina didn't talk to the press." Leo's cruel, brilliant eyes fell on Tali's face. "It is what *Papà* wanted."

Tali choked on a breath. How could he be so vicious, so inhumane? This wasn't even about sex. It was all just about the stupid press. My God, how could she have been so stupid?

"Fine. Then send the woman away already. I'll handle Vincenzo Romano. He's a cantankerous old bird, but he's not stupid. If he's dying, he needs the deal done as much as us." The two brothers, gorgeous, arrogant, and intimidating, stared at each other like gladiators. "And I'll drag him through the courts if that's what has to happen."

"Go home, Mariano, and don't tell me what I must do. Take care of your problems and leave me to handle my own."

Tali found her voice. She didn't recognize the flat, controlled tone that came out of her. "For your information, I never spoke to the press, and I don't give a flying pig anymore if you believe me or not. But it's the truth."

"We know," Leo informed her from behind his desk. "It was the security guard to whom you told the story."

"We should have known. Looking at you now, I would

never believe you to be that smart." Mariano's words were filled with disdain.

Tali's temper flared white hot—hot enough to burn down the whole house. She snorted. "You listen here, bonehead!" She pointed an index finger at Mariano's face. Behind him, Tali noticed Leonardo close his eyes and shake his head. But he didn't stop her. "I don't need protection from you. I may not be the brightest crayon in the box, but I can take what you think of me, wrap it in compost, and use it as fertilizer." And to finish her point, she raised her leg and stepped on Mariano's perfect designer shoe as hard as possible.

Mariano swore as he removed his shoe and massaged his toes. His face turned beet red. "*Che Diavolo*? You are nuts!"

Ignoring Mariano's pained expression, Tali fixed her sight on Leonardo. "As for you, you knew it wasn't me who sold the story, and you didn't even apologize to me?" If ever there was a time to scream, that time was now. But Tali didn't have the strength. The weight of the world had fallen on her shoulders. Exhaustion rolled over her. "You lied to me over and over again. You brought me here with a lie, and you have the guts to call me dishonest? I hate you!"

"I only found out a few weeks ago, Talisman. It wasn't like I knew it from the beginning."

"You've known for weeks?" She meant nothing to him but a problem requiring a solution. A severe cramp pierced Tali's lower stomach. She covered her abdomen with both hands. Another stabbing contraction forced a wail out of her. And then she saw the blood. What was happening? She looked at Leo, and he was ashen. She'd never seen him so pale. "Leo, help me."

"Talisman?" Leo's otherwise sharp, controlled voice thickened and trembled. "*No, Dio, no. No, per favore*!" He reached her in time to catch her in his arms as her vision faded to black.

Chapter Twelve

Leo leaned over the black wrought-iron railing of the catwalk that looked over his home's extensive living area. Past midnight, a mournful stillness prevailed. This mansion was an imitation of himself, an empty shell. He destroyed everything he touched, and now he had killed his child. He fastened his fingers on the railing until the skin of his knuckles whitened.

The doctor's sympathetic words bounced like rubber balls in Leo's head. "A miscarriage is common during the first trimester of pregnancy. Neither of you did anything wrong." The doctor wasn't there to see how he'd treated Tali or the stress he'd caused her. In the absence of his mother, Leo had punished Talisman for Agustina's mistake.

Leo frowned, remembering Tali's face in the hospital. Up until the last moment, she'd held out for good news. He saw it in her eyes. But the glow of optimism she managed to carry with her, no matter how dismal the circumstances, faded with the doctor's explanation. She'd demanded that Leo leave her alone, and he'd complied. He'd left the room but stayed in the hospital, wandering the halls like a ghost. He should've stayed with her. A worthy man would have never let her face their horrible loss by herself. But he was a devious, deceptive man. A shell of a man without a heart or selfless affection for others. He'd ignored his feelings for many years. Perhaps he'd managed to destroy them.

He brought Tali home the following day with the doctor's recommendation that she rest for another week. How could he take care of her when he was the cause of her loss and pain? He should've never brought her to this place. But he wanted to be with her and let his lust overrule his common sense. He had lied to her and to himself.

His actions appalled him now. He'd displayed the behavior of an arrogant bastard from the first day they'd met. He'd always been arrogant, and that had never bothered him before. He was damaged goods. Some people understood and forgave him, and others didn't care. But Tali had endured the brunt of it. *Dio Mio,* he'd used her feelings and confusion against her.

The night she gave him her body, she'd given him her heart. If he were a man of any honor, he'd have sent her away when he recognized her feelings for him. But he was a man without integrity. In his self-centered way, he'd kept her with him. He told himself that it was for his family. But how often had his brother and father told him to send her away? Neither Mariano nor Fausto would approve of his actions. No, he'd done it for himself. He desired Tali. And whatever Leonardo Guerranti wanted, he made sure to have it.

Leo rubbed a hand over his face. He had to find a way to fix this horrible mess. Tali refused to discuss the miscarriage. Dark spots under her eyes and an unhealthy, pasty complexion were his daily reminder of their tragedy. He missed her smiles, the sparkle in her eyes, and her saucy opinions. She insisted on returning to New York as soon as possible. Not having her with him was unthinkable. What the hell was wrong with him?

How different would his life have been had he grown up with a loving mother? What kind of mother sold her baby, leaving him in the hands of cruel people? He owed her nothing. While other kids' grandparents spoiled them, Leo's grandparents showed him a harsh and unsympathetic attitude. He spent his younger years mitigating his heartache through rebellion by living on the edge. His father cared, but he kept a distance between them. Fausto had a different relationship with Mariano. They had more in common.

What did it matter now? He couldn't even keep his child or Tali safe. Leo's stomach twisted. There was nothing he could do now about the miscarriage, or how he'd treated her in the past. But what about the promise he'd made her? Did he have the courage to face his demons?

Was there a possibility that Agustina Rossi had changed? Did she repent of her past behavior the way he regretted his own mistakes? Did Agustina miss him the way he missed his child? His baby never had the opportunity to live, but knowing they'd existed had forced a change in Leo. He'd fathered a child. Agustina had carried him in her belly, felt him grow, and given birth to him. Did she regret giving him up? Had she tried to contact him when he was still a child? No, his father would have told him. He rubbed the back of his neck. What if he was setting himself up for another disappointment? Agustina could be the same greedy creature who'd sold him and left Italy without giving him a second thought. For most of his life, he'd believed people were unable and unwilling to change. They learned to hide their flaws. Now he wasn't so sure.

Leo took a deep breath. Was he betraying his father if he called Agustina? Fausto was not a perfect father by anyone's standards. But he was present in Leo's life. He supported him and loved him, which was more than Leo could say about his mother. His father would be hurt and betrayed by that call. However, this decision was of minor consequence to Fausto compared to what it meant for Leo. Yes, he had made Tali a promise, one he'd never intended to fulfill when he made it. The past few months' events, culminating in the loss of his child, had changed everything. He didn't know how or why it had happened, but it had. He'd hidden his pain behind a tough-guy façade. He'd believed his lie until Talisman crashed into his life. She tore open old wounds, but she'd also showed him the possibility of a different life. Now he needed to find out if it was all real or another fantasy.

If he'd been correct all this time, and Agustina was still the same greedy woman of thirty-five years ago, he'd be free to put a lid on that box and never open it again. But what if she had changed? Was there a possibility of healing those old wounds? He peeped down one hall. Tali's door was closed, just as he'd left it after delivering her dinner hours earlier. With the time difference, it was past 6 PM in New York. He rushed downstairs, taking the steps two at a time. Leo didn't want to wait one more minute now that he'd decided to open the door to his past. He locked himself in his office.

Leo found Agustina's contact information within the digital file Matteo had sent him months ago. He took his mobile phone and dialed the number. A woman answered. Leo's tongue tasted like sand and was just as dry. He glanced at the bar. He should have poured himself a drink before making the call. Too late now.

He licked his lips. "Is this Agustina Rossi?" Part of him hoped it was a wrong number.

"Yes, this is Agustina," she replied in Italian. Did she know it was him? Of course not. What was he thinking?

"*Signora* Rossi, this is Leonardo Guerranti. Can we talk?" His belly stiffened into a ball of nerves. What if she said no? There were two or three endless seconds of silence. Then a burst of sobs came through loud and clear.

"My son, is it you?" Understanding Agustina's rushed words was a challenge as she sobbed into the phone. "My boy, my son, please tell me it really is you. I've prayed and hoped that you'd call me."

Leo's vision blurred. He brushed the tears off his cheeks with the back of his hand. His lungs burned from the effort to keep a semblance of control.

"Mamma..."

Two days later...

Tali lifted the lid off the big pot on the stove. Her stomach growled as the familiar toasty scent of gumbo filled her nostrils. "Oh yeah, it smells just like my momma's gumbo!" She hadn't been hungry since her miscarriage. Noemi, the chef, stood by her side, watching the simmering stew.

She'd spent a week in her bedroom since coming back from the hospital. A week thinking about the loss of her baby. A week coming to terms with the horrible things that came out of Leo's mouth just before the miscarriage. He'd been deliberately cruel. Was that his way to get back at her for what she'd told him at the festival about exchanging one mother for another? He'd stopped visiting her room, as he'd done every day since returning from the hospital, taking her meals and ensuring she ate them. When she did see him, he was distracted and in a bad mood.

Tali had pushed Leo away as she mourned their baby, but that was his own danged fault. She didn't blame him for the miscarriage, though he blamed himself. She saw how it tortured him and how hard he worked to hide his feelings from her. She'd needed to see his vulnerabilities, but he had none. He had the hardness of cold marble, even in grief. Tali didn't want to wallow in her pain but shutting it away wasn't the answer either. That's what she'd done when her parents died, leading to a deeper world of hurt. Leo's reaction was proof that he'd never change. He'd never be the open, honest, loving soulmate she needed. Tali did a mental shake of her thoughts. She was ready to live in the present again.

"You write the recipe for me, *si*?" Noemi watched over Tali's shoulder as she stirred the soup and took a bay leaf out of the pot.

"*Si*! This is my momma's recipe." Tali smiled at the older woman. It was a pleasure to show this excellent cook how to make her momma's gumbo. "I hope you'll like it."

She was going home, no matter what Leo said. Not to New York. She was returning to Louisiana to make a life for herself again in the place she was born. Her heart ached for Isola Rosalia. She'd come to think of this place as home in a short time. The people were kind and welcoming. She liked visiting the local market and making groceries with Bianca and her mom, helping the gardeners, or passing a good time with the guards. They were not as intimidating as she'd first thought.

And then there was Leo. Whether they were sailing, swimming, exploring the island, or watching TV, she enjoyed her time with him when he wasn't being a total numskull. He'd introduced her to a world of sensuality, always leaving her wanting more. She'd fallen in love with him, holding on to a small flame of hope.

Leo had extinguished her spark when she heard the cruel way in which he informed his brother of his true intentions toward her. Was it pride? Dignity? Whatever happened had given her the strength to stand up for herself. This little game she'd allowed him to play with her for months was over. He never intended to speak with his momma. That was a lie. A trap to get her to do what he wanted.

Tali dipped a spoon in the gumbo, blew on the steamy liquid to cool it, and tasted it. She grinned at Noemi. Taking another spoon, Tali scooped more soup. "It is good. Here, try it."

Noemi tasted the gumbo and nodded with enthusiasm. She opened her mouth to speak, but loud male voices reached the kitchen. The women turned to the door at the same time. There was more shouting, Leo's voice more piercing than the others.

Tali turned off the stove and wiped her hands on her apron. "Stay here, ladies." Noemi and Bianca nodded. "I'll go see what's happening." She left the apron on the kitchen table and followed the sound of angry voices.

She found Leo, Mariano, and Fausto in the foyer, near the elegant double curved stairs. The older man kept his back hunched over, his chin so close to resting on his chest that an onlooker might think he was asleep. Leo had his back to her, but judging by how his neck muscles strained tighter than the cords of a guitar and the wide stance of his long legs, she knew his fury boiled over.

"Tali, how are you?" Mariano strode past Leonardo, who stopped talking to stare at her. Leo's gray eyes were cold as icebergs, but Mariano looked pleased to see her and offered her his hand. Perhaps it was a trick of the light that made Mariano's honey-colored eyes glisten with something like concern. Tali didn't trust him, but she shook his hand to stop the fight.

"I'm doing much better, thank you." She angled her lips into a half-smile. That was the best she could do.

Fausto put a hand on Leo's shoulder, but the younger man jerked away from his father's touch. "*Mi scuso, Leonardo. Mi dispiace molto di averti mentito.*"

"You're sorry?" Leo hollered back in English. "You're sorry for lying to me? I don't think so, *Pappà*. You're sorry for getting caught!" Leo marched to the front door and pushed it open. "Now leave."

Mariano stood between the two men. "Leonardo, that's enough."

Leo shut the door again with a bang. "But of course you're taking his side. I should've expected that."

"What in the Sam Hill is going on here?" Tali looked from one man to another. What had happened to cause Leo to speak that way to his father?

Mariano spoke first. "Who is Sam Hill?"

Really? That was what he wanted to know right now? Tali

opened her mouth to explain, but Leo interrupted her.

"No, no, no! We're not going there again." He put up a hand. "Apparently Sam Hill is a guy who used to swear a lot." He turned to Talisman. "What's going on is that I finally know the truth about what happened to my mother."

"How did you find out? Your father—?"

"No, my father only admitted the truth when circumstances forced him to do so." He paced the empty foyer like a caged animal. "I called Agustina a couple of days ago."Talisman's shock couldn't have been greater had she seen an alien ship land in the garden. So that was why Leo was acting so weird the last two days. But why hadn't he said anything?

Fausto was an older version of Leonardo. His cloudy gray eyes examined Tali for a moment. "My parents threatened to have Agustina's parents arrested and sent to prison for theft if she didn't give Leo up. But of course, you know that much already."

He looked fragile, ready to fall to the ground at any minute. Tali rushed to his side.

"I'm okay. You're a good girl. You don't deserve to be in the middle of this. My grandparents had great influence in Italy and enough money to get away with anything. They'd have had her parents arrested for theft unless the family moved away from Italy for good and left me here." Leo pushed Mariano's arm away when his brother tried to soothe him. "And you lied to me for thirty-five years! What sort of man does that to his child?"

"I loved your mother. I was embarrassed for not standing up to my parents to defend her." Fausto's flat voice was suddenly thickened by emotion. He turned to Tali like a drowning man turned to driftwood for support in the middle of the ocean. "I loved her...and I still do."

"Stop lying to me and spare me the sentimentality blackmail!"

Tali flinched as Leo's voice rumbled like thunder throughout the house. Leo had the right to be furious, as she knew he would be once he learned the truth. But she refused to sit back one more second and allow him to act all high and mighty, as if he were perfect himself. Besides, watching the color drain from Mariano's face, she thought he was a perfect physical match for Leonardo and looked ready to throw the first punch.

Mariano's deep, sharp growl thickened the strained situation close to the breaking point. "You'd better start showing respect for *Papà* before I make you eat your words."

Leo swerved in his brother's direction. "You want to fight me? Fine, I'm right here, *fratello*." He squared his shoulders and glared at Mariano.

"I'm ready to teach you to have some compassion for the man who raised you." A nerve on Mariano's jaw pulsed wildly.

Leo let out a loud laugh. "You think you can teach me compassion? You? The spoilt brat? Where's your compassion for Gianna? You were ready and willing to throw her under the bus for a business deal."

Tali stepped between the brothers. "Enough!" This was not how she'd hoped things would happen. "Leo, you have the right to be angry at your father, but you don't have the right to talk like you're all perfect, either." Heat crept up from Tali's belly. How dare he behave like he'd done nothing wrong himself? He was no better than his father, the way he'd treated her all this time. "My God, you'll never change. You lied to me to convince me to come here with you. You only called your mother because you felt guilty. Now you know the truth, and you're ready to punish your father?" She put a hand on Leo's chest and pushed him hard until his back was against the wall. "You're a smug jerk. Do you know what I'd give to have my parents alive?"

"Talisman, stop. You're still recovering from the miscarriage." Leo wrapped a hand around Tali's arm. "You should be in bed, resting."

"Oh, you're good." She pulled away from him. "Do not touch me again. And you are not responsible for my miscarriage. That was an accident. Yes, I've heard you pacing the house all night long. All that guilt you're carrying is what made you call your mother. The world doesn't revolve around you, especially not my world." That was an outright lie, but he deserved to be brought down a few pegs.

Fausto spoke from the other side of the foyer. "Leo's right, Talisman. He's right about everything. I'm sorry, son. I was afraid of telling you the truth because I knew you'd never forgive me."

Tali turned to Fausto. She'd had enough of this pity party. "And you, sir, need to face your mistakes. You owe Agustina a debt you can never repay. You kept her son from her for thirty-five years and taught him to hate her. Figure out a way to make amends."

Mariano was leaning against the front door, his arms folded over his chest. His golden-brown eyes were not missing a thing. Pushing her chin forward, Tali challenged him to say something, anything. But he maintained an impenetrable expression. Only his intense, brilliant eyes showed signs of life.

She turned her eyes back to Leonardo. He kept his hands twisted into tight fists. His nostrils flared. He was learning to cope with the awful pain of parental betrayal. All she wanted to do was run into his arms, kiss him, and tell him she was on his side. How could she still be so stupid, knowing he didn't give a damn about her? Knowing that everything he did was a trap, a ruse to get her to agree to his plans. There was one reason—she loved him with everything in her. His pain was her pain.

Leo was selfish enough to let her stay and comfort him, which to him only meant sex, of course. He was in pain now, but he was also a self-centered brute. Leo had used her and taken everything she gave him. Yes, he was hurting now. His father had betrayed him and his brother did not defend him. The people for whom he'd be willing to do anything—even marry a woman he didn't love—had let him down. But Leonardo Guerranti was a fighter, and he'd get past this bump on the road. He didn't need her. She had to leave now.

"I want to go home. I'm leaving this island today, one way or another. Give me my documents. I don't want to stay here one more night." She looked Leonardo straight in the eyes. If only he loved her a little, enough to ask her to stay. Tali refused to ask herself if she'd stay. What was the point? He didn't need her here anymore. The scandal of their fake marriage had died down. The media had fresher stories to keep them occupied. He knew his mother had not sold him to his father and that she wouldn't sell their story either. And their child hadn't survived. She never got to see their little face in a sonogram. There was no reason for Leo to keep her in his house.

"If that's what you want, it will be done. My helicopter will take you to Rome, and you can take my plane back to New York. I'll have everything ready by this evening." He didn't even try to stop her. Obviously, he believed their time together had come to an end. Tali's heart shattered. How could he be so cold?

"No, have someone drive me to the village. I'll make my way home." She didn't want to spend one hour more than necessary at Isola Rosalia.

"Talisman," Mariano interrupted the conversation. "Please, allow my father and me to fly you to the mainland. We can leave as soon as you're ready to go."

"Always the perfect gentleman, aren't you, *fratello*?" Tart hostility dripped from Leo's voice. He looked at Tali. "I'll have Bianca deliver your documents to your room. I'm sure you want to get out of here as soon as possible. Living with me in this place had to be pure hell for you, *arcobaleno*." Without another word, Leonardo marched in the direction of his office. The open wound in Tali's heart bled for him. She'd get over that man if it was the last thing she did. Tali took Mariano up on his offer and ran upstairs to pack.

She collected her things in less than fifteen minutes. She was taking only what she'd brought with her. All the other stuff—clothes and gifts Leo had bought for her—were part of a fantasy that had ended worse than Tali had ever imagined. She'd fallen in love with the wrong man, and he'd broken her heart.

Tali looked at her disheveled image in the mirror. She'd made the same mistakes as her mother. She fell for a man who prioritized his needs and wants before his family. This was the truth she refused to face all these years. She loved her daddy over everything else, and his death had allowed her to forget his faults. She'd put him on a pedestal and judged every man by those standards. But her parents were not perfect. Her daddy's need to change the world and leave his mark on it allowed him to put his family in second place without remorse. Her momma pretended everything was terrific and taught Tali the same way. She never demanded to be first in anyone's life because she'd been taught it was selfish to feel that way.

How could she accept that Leo had been willing to sacrifice a part of himself to help his brother but refused to reconcile with his mother? She saw an unforgiving man who declined to give another person the opportunity they needed and desired. Why had she fought so hard to reunite Agustina with her son? Part of it was because she loved her friend, but there was a deeper, darker reason, one that satisfied her wish to reunite herself with her parents. She wasn't as selfless and humanitarian as she pretended to be. And then she'd met Leo, and all generosity and self-sacrificing ideals went out the window. She'd come to this place because she'd fallen for him like a sex-crazed teenager, and then she fell in love with him.

This fantasy was over. Leo did not love her back. How could he? She was still the flat-broke inadequate woman he took to his bed because she allowed him to. She fit into his life like a bag of coffee in a tea shop.

Tali fixed her hair and makeup. Bianca delivered her documents, and the two women hugged each other. At least she'd made a new friend. They promised to stay in touch. Downstairs, Mariano grabbed her bag and led her to the helicopter, where Fausto waited for them.

Tali looked around at the garden and the beach in the distance. She'd miss this place. Leo did not come out to say goodbye. She meant nothing to him. This episode of his life was over, and he'd moved on without a second thought. Minutes later, the helicopter took her away.

Chapter Thirteen

New Orleans, two months later…

Leo stepped out of his hotel onto busy Canal Street and studied the GPS directions on his phone. November daylight faded quickly in New Orleans, but the city was lit up and ready for the upcoming Thanksgiving Day festivities. He was fifteen minutes away from Jackson Square, less if he walked at a fast pace. He dashed past ornamental railings, carriages pulled by elegant horses, musicians playing on sidewalks. Tali's shift ended in twenty minutes. He could not afford to miss her. She'd be more agreeable in public…he hoped.

Leo hastened past the statue of the American president Andrew Jackson on his horse. He sat on the edge of the circular water fountain, fixing his attention on a restaurant across the street. Leo had spent two months planning this day. Everything had to be perfect. He often picked up the phone to call her, but he had to give her time. Time to regain her independence, gather her thoughts, and miss him. She loved him, and he adored her. They were meant for each other. She was his soulmate.

When he'd met Talisman, his life had changed in ways he'd never expected. Everything Leo believed about himself, about his family, got turned on its ear. Before asking her to believe he was the man she'd been searching for, he'd had to fix himself. She was his good luck charm and he was her shield…her protection in this life.

He'd refused to say goodbye the day she'd left Isola Rosalia. He had to regroup, to think of a way to get her back. That was why he'd locked himself in his office. He wasn't letting her go. This was temporary. The night he'd spoken on the phone with his mother, Leo had admitted to himself that he was wholly and hopelessly in love with Talisman. He planned to tell her so and beg her to stay with him. But his brother and father had shown up and shattered his plan. In hindsight, things happened the way they had to happen. He'd kept her like a prisoner for weeks. He'd lied to her, manipulated her. She'd never have believed him if he had confessed his love for her then. But enough time had passed—she had to listen to him now. He'd find a way to convince her that his love was real, honest, and pure. He had to apologize for the terrible things he'd done to her. The last time he saw her, dignity and pride made her appear larger than life, like a queen. His pocket-sized Talisman had grown into her own, and he was proud of her. Proud of the way she stood up to him and to his family.

Out of the corner of his eye, he noticed a flash of color. Tali's long purple braid swayed from side to side. She wore a peach sweater and flowy red pants. He jumped to his feet and ignored the annoyed drivers as he raced across the street before she could disappear into the crowd. Leo was close enough to touch her when Talisman stopped and swung in his direction.

She opened her lips and shut them again without a word. She fixed the focus of her sparkling turquoise eyes on him.

He recognized fear, excitement, and surprise. He shuddered to think Tali might fear him. "Talisman, we need to talk." Not the most brilliant or original phrase, but it was better than standing frozen in place. She didn't say a word. As if he wasn't there, she pivoted and walked away. He ran to her, grabbed her arm. "Tali, please. I need to talk to you." She pulled away and kept moving. Fine, he was willing to walk to the ends of the Earth. It had to be a shock to find him there after not hearing a peep from him since she left the island. But he wasn't giving up. "You can walk as much as you want. I'll follow you until you hear me out."

She stopped and watched him with guarded eyes. "Whatever you want to say, I don't want to hear it." The fear had disappeared, and Leo found his breath again. Good, this was more like the Tali he knew and understood.

"Yes, you do." It was now or never. He had to show her he was telling the truth. "I love you, Talisman." People stopped to gawk at them.

"Liar! What's your game now?" Tali pulled on the strap of her bag, which had slid down her arm when she came to a sudden halt.

"No game, no lies. Just the truth." Leo's stomach clenched and churned. He ached to take her in his arms and kiss her. That was all he'd thought about for two months. He kept his arms by his sides and waited. He was prepared to wait for her as long as it took.

Tali scoffed. "You lied to me from the beginning. I hoped for so long I was wrong and that you were not just using me." She shook her head. "But then I heard what you told your brother. I'm nothing but a problem, one that you were handling, remember? You told him I mean nothing to you."

Now it was Leo's turn to shake his head. "Mariano can be vicious. I didn't want him to hurt you. I had to lie to him to protect you. But he knows the truth now. Everybody knows that I'm in love with you." The crowd around them uttered noises of disapproval.

One of the artists selling his work on the street chuckled. "Brother, you're gonna hafta do better than that, 'cause ain't nobody here on your side right now."

Leo frowned at the man. "I made many mistakes with this woman, but I love her more than life itself."

Tali glanced at the artist. "No, he doesn't. He used me, and he dumped me." There were more oohs from the crowd.

"I never dumped her." Leo closed the distance between himself and Tali. "I never dumped you. I let you go because you asked me to let you go."

"I gave you an out, and you jumped on it." A streak of crimson stained her cheeks. "You didn't even say goodbye. You couldn't *wait* to get rid of me."

Leo drew a deep breath as the familiar scents of jasmine and vanilla filled his nostrils. "Do you know why I didn't see you off?" She opened her mouth, but Leo brushed it with the tip of his index finger. "Because it wasn't goodbye. You needed time away from me and everything that happened between us. You weren't ready to believe how much I love you." He stared into her eyes, wishing she could read the truth in his face. She made one of her many faces, rolling her eyes and making a tsk sound with her tongue. "Fine, you don't believe me? Watch this."

With a quick movement, and showing off his terrific physical shape, Leo jumped over the railing separating a café from the narrow sidewalk and stood on top of a small, round table. People took out their mobile phones. A waiter ordered him to climb off the table, but he ignored the man. "My name is Leonardo Guerranti." He locked his eyes on Tali's face. He hoped she remembered their breakfast at the trattoria and her little speech. Two could play the same game. "I love Talisman Broussard, the gorgeous woman over there." He pointed at her. "The one with the long, purple braid. I did wrong by her, and I will always be sorry. All I want is a chance to prove to her that I am the love of her life. Talisman, please, talk to me. Listen to me, *arcobaleno. Per favore.*" People cheered. He finally had the crowd on his side.

"Fine!" Talisman pressed her lips and crossed her arms over her chest, but Leo refused to move. One word wasn't enough. He waited. "Fine, I'll listen to whatever you want to say. But not here." The crowd clapped. He jumped off the table and vaulted to the other side of the railing.

A woman in the crowd hollered at Leo to make it count or the girl would put a *gris-gris* on him. He intended to do that, even if he had no clue what *gris-gris* meant. His life and his future depended on this. He approached Tali and held her hand. "We can talk anywhere you want."

"I live in the Marigny, fifteen minutes from here on foot." They headed up Decatur Street, holding hands. She didn't pull away, and Leo considered that a small victory. He missed the softness of her skin, the way his body tingled when they touched. He had a second chance and did not intend to waste it.

"What got into you tonight? People are gonna upload videos of you standing on that table. There's bound to be yet another scandal online," she scolded him.

"I'm used to it by now. And I learned this technique from the best." He grinned when she groaned and rolled her eyes. "By the way, what's *gris-gris*?"

"Oh, that? It's a Cajun word for a curse, like in voodoo." A flash of mischievousness crossed Tali's attractive features. She flashed him an evil look.

A warm feeling crawled up Leo's body. His funny, irreverent Tali was still there, hiding behind layers of pride and fear. He had to get through those layers and prove that she'd been right. She did have a soulmate waiting for her, and now he was here. He gripped her hand a little tighter and kept walking in silence.

They stopped in front of a narrow yellow house with white trimming, a blue door, a blue window, a gabled roof, and a tiny front porch. Leo would have recognized it anywhere, having spent a long time studying it in photos and videos. They stood on the small front porch as Tali searched her purse for her keys. Her hands trembled but she managed to insert the key in the hole and opened the door.

The house was narrow and long, resembling a bowling alley. Inside near the entrance were two colorful sofas. A yellow area rug set off the living room. The dining area was marked by a wooden table with six chairs in bright assorted colors. The whole place had a bohemian feel—sunny, colorful, and happy. This house was the personification of the woman he loved. Was it any wonder he felt at home at once?

"The bathroom's in the back, next to the kitchen." Tali closed the front door and tossed her bag on one of the sofas, but she didn't sit.

Leo glanced around the room. "Thank you, but I'm all right." The place was small, but everything in it screamed Tali. "So, this is a shotgun house." He made a statement, not a question. Leo recognized his mistake at once.

"Yes, but how did you…?" Tali frowned. She widened her eyes. "Wait a minute. Did you have something to do with me getting this place at such a low rent?"

Leo rubbed the back of his neck. *Here we go.* His first opportunity at the whole honesty thing. "I spoke with the owner and offered to pay him the rest of the rent and a bit more if he kept it between us." He wanted to be honest about everything, even the most minor details.

Tali pointed a finger at him. "You had no right to do that! Who the hell do you think you are? What about my waitressing job? Did you get me that too?"

"I love you and will always look out for you." He reached to touch her cheek. She pulled back from him. "I'd never hurt you, *arcobaleno*. I called the owner of the café and put in a good word for you. He kept you on the job because you're a good waitress, but I hope you won't stay there long."

"You don't love me. Stop saying that." She stood near the dining table, putting space between them. "You feel guilty over the miscarriage, that's all. Please leave." She moved her gaze to the ground. "And stop having me followed."

Leo crossed the room and stood next to Tali. He wasn't walking away again. "I do feel guilty, but it isn't about the miscarriage. I will always miss our baby. But my guilt is over the way I treated you." He closed his eyes for a moment. He'd been so blind, so stupid. "I recognized you when I first saw you in my office in New York. Not the conventional way, but in my gut and my heart." He looked deep into her eyes, trying to read her thoughts. "You felt it too, Talisman. I know you did."

Tali narrowed her eyes. "You threw me out of your office and had me arrested." Her voice held a note of condemnation—he deserved it.

"Yes, and I'm sorry for that." He gave her a sheepish little smile. "But I had the charges dropped right away."

She insisted on talking about stuff he hadn't considered in ages. "You ignored my calls and told the staff to keep me out of your office." How much resentment did she harbor against him? "You took me away with a lie and didn't care that I was losing my job, my home, everything. You *never* cared."

He softened his lips into a little smile again. "But Tali, don't you see?"

She shook her head. "See what?"

"I tried to keep you away because of the thunderbolt I felt right here." He touched his chest. "I felt it the first time we met, and I've never felt anything like that. Never!" He wanted to be open and vulnerable to earn the chance to be believed.

She shook her head. "It's too late, Leonardo. I don't want to have an affair with you until you get tired of having me around. I'm worth much more than being your flavor of the month."

Her words couldn't hurt more than if she'd sucker-punched him in the stomach. This was another reminder of how much he'd hurt her, all the pain he'd caused her. He earned every word of hostility she threw in his direction, and it also gave him hope. She wouldn't feel this way if she didn't love him still.

"Let me prove to you that it isn't too late. Our love *is* worth the fight." Wild horses couldn't drag him away from here tonight. He'd even taken the precaution of turning off his phone while waiting at Jackson Square. "I don't pretend to be that guy trying to save the world. I'm not like your dad, and probably never will be, but I've been waiting for you my entire life. I've never been in love before. I'm thirty-five years old and I never fell in love until I met you. Do you know why?" He ran the back of his hand over her cheek. "For the same reason that you never fell in love at twenty-six years of age until you met me. We're meant for each other, *arcobaleno*. Can't you forgive my stupidity, *per favore*?" She was so close, inches away.

He lowered his head and brushed his mouth against Tali's. His heart pounded so hard, so loud, Leo was sure she could hear it. She opened her lips, and he tasted her again. Electricity shot through him. He held his woman in his arms and she sparked life in every cell of his body. He'd been in limbo for two months, not dead but not alive either. Nothing mattered to him more than this woman and this moment in time.

Tali froze. What was she doing? She was falling for his tricks again. She pushed at Leo's chest. Her hand flew across the air and smashed against his cheek. He probably thought she'd been longing for him all this time. She had, but that wasn't the point. The gall of the man. Did he think she was so desperate for him that she'd fall at his feet, sick with love, like some romance heroine from centuries ago because he arrived with pretty words of love?

He stepped back, massaging the cheek she'd slapped. Anguish and astonishment flashed over his face, then disappeared, leaving bruised skin and a pitiful expression.

Good. She only wished she'd been one of those women who spent all day at the gym. She might've loosened some of his teeth. "Why are you doing all of this? Have you lost your mind?" She held back the desire to caress the red flesh on his cheek.

He fell back onto the edge of the sofa.

"You don't need to concern yourself with me anymore. Why are you really here? You want to torture me some more?"

Leo sat down and stretched his long legs. He leaned over, resting his head on his hands. He kept silent so long that Tali dropped onto the other sofa. This was not the same man with whom she'd lived at Isola Rosalia. She thought he'd moved on, relieved to be rid of her, only to find out he'd been keeping track of her, helping her get on with her life like some weird guardian angel. This was remorse, nothing more. He wanted to make amends for how he'd treated her, for the loss of their baby. Leonardo Guerranti loved himself and his family. He'd never fall in love with a woman like her. He'd made this abundantly clear in London. He offered her a one-night stand and nothing else. Her stay at Isola Rosalia was a strange fluke, never meant to happen. They were born for each other as much as a bird and a fish. She was not letting him sweet-talk her into spending the night together. She was worth a hell of a lot more than to be a man's plaything.

"The night of the festival, you accused me of replacing Agustina with Mariano's mother." The pain in his voice surprised her. "She despised me, Talisman." His gaze fell back on her face. "It's okay, you didn't know. I tried to get close, but she was a vicious woman. I think my father married her to atone for his sins against my mother."

"I'm sorry." There was so much more she wanted to say. But that meant risking her heart again, and that was one thing

Tali refused to do.

"I grew up rebelling against the idea of love. Not because I didn't believe in it, but because I didn't want to get hurt...and I didn't want to be rejected again. Even my grandparents told me I was the bastard son of a maid and I was lucky to be accepted into their family. I grew up knowing I had to prove myself worthy of the Guerranti name." His voice thickened. The edges of his mouth twitched in a sad smile.

Tali's heart constricted and squirmed in her breast. Why was he opening up to her now? What did he want from her this time? She wasn't falling for his manipulations again. He'd taught her a painful lesson. She'd never forget or forgive him. She did what she'd set out to do, reunite him with his mother. Her time at Isola Rosalia was over. She was no longer the silly girl who thought she could save the world. Now she knew there was no such thing as a soulmate. He'd forced her to take a long, hard look at herself and admit certain truths about her life. There was no going back now.

"I don't blame you. Love can hurt you. Even destroy you." She pressed her lips into a forced smile. "You mentioned earlier that you'd never be like my father."

He nodded.

"Good. The truth is that my dad always put his causes before my mother and me. He loved us, but he didn't think twice about leaving us for months while he was off saving some part of the world." Her jaw trembled and the back of her eyes burned as memories of her parents rushed back to her. "The night we crashed, they argued because he wanted to leave again. He wasn't paying attention to the road. That's why he didn't see the drunk driver until it was too late. I idealized him and used him as a yardstick with which to compare all other men. But the yardstick wasn't real, because my image of Momma and Daddy wasn't real."

"He also did many fun things with your mother and you.

You never went hungry, and he kept a roof over your heads. Don't let the lousy memories overshadow the wonderful ones."

How odd to hear those words come from Leonardo.

He smiled. "A smart woman called me a smug jerk not long ago and reminded me the world doesn't revolve around me. I learned that forgiveness is about releasing the bad and making room for the good."

So now she was taking lessons on forgiveness from Leonardo Guerranti? Had the world flipped on its ear? Had she falled through a rabbit hole and landed in some freaky dimension? "I'm not the same person I was when we met."

"My love, you're the person you were always meant to be." A touch of a glimmer animated his gray eyes. "You're brilliant, opinionated, brave, caring, marvelous. You're daring, and your temper flares at the drop of a hat."

She shot off the sofa like a cannon. How dare Leo claim she had a bad temper? "I do *not* have a temper," she shouted at him. "Tell me one time when I showed a bad temper!"

"When I had to fix the doors of my kitchen cupboards. The times you slapped me." He touched his face. "When you called my brother a bonehead—"

"Whatever, shut up." She marched to the kitchen. His raucous laughter followed her. Blood surged throughout her body. She'd missed his laugh more than she wanted to admit. "I'm hungry."

"So? What else is new?" She nearly jumped out of her skin when she heard his voice next to her ear. How was he behind her and she hadn't noticed?

"I was going to offer you some leftover jambalaya, but now you can forget it." She took the casserole out of the fridge and placed it on the counter.

"I've never had jambalaya." He sniffed the air a couple of times. "It smells good. Did you cook it?"

Tali rolled her eyes. "Yes. And fine, you can eat some. Get

the bowls and utensils. They're in that cabinet." She pointed with her head as she twisted a button to light a burner on the stove.

They sat across from each other on colorful chairs around the dining table. Tali served the jambalaya into each bowl and filled two glasses with water. She wasn't in the habit of buying wine.

"This food is delicious." He spoke between bites. "*Mamma* is staying on the island with me, by the way."

"Thank you." Hearing him refer to Agustina as *mamma* made her want to smile. She took a big bite of her food to stop herself. "That's good."

"She and *Papà* are getting along well." He paused for a moment and frowned. "I think something's happening there, but they're not telling."

"Does that upset you?" Was a former maid not good enough for his dear old *papà*, even if it was Leo's mother?

He sipped his water. "Not at all. I'd love to see my parents together and happy."

"Then why the frown?"

"I was just thinking, what if they get married before us?"

Tali choked on her water. Was he out of his silly little mind? "You and I are never getting married."

Leo grunted, but thank goodness he dropped the subject. They spent the next hour eating dinner and cleaning up. How easy it became to fall back into their old routine from when the staff at Isola Rosalia had days off.

But Tali wasn't ready to believe this sudden love Leo professed. There had to be another reason for him to show up now. Maybe his brother's business deal hadn't happened. Perhaps they still blamed her for everything going down the way it had. Of course, now they knew it wasn't Tali who sold the fake news story about their wedding. But the story wouldn't have become an issue if she hadn't blabbed her lie to the security guard.

"Did something happen to Mariano's business deal?" They were back in the living room with two tall glasses of sweet tea.

"No, he's handling it." Something about the way he said that sent shivers down Tali's spine. Didn't Leo approve of what his brother was doing? This was not her problem. "Why do you ask?"

"Just trying to figure out why you're here." She crossed her legs underneath her.

"Listen, Tali, I'm here for you, only you. I'm your man. You're my woman. It took me a little longer to realize it, but I did." He crossed the room and pulled her to her feet. "You love me, damn it. You love me, and I adore you."

She tried to shake her head, but all she achieved was a weak slight tremor. "No, I don't—" She couldn't say it. She couldn't say she didn't love him.

"Liar," he whispered in her ear. "You can't finish that sentence."

Sparks of electricity flickered through her body. He entwined his arms around her shoulders, pulled her closer. A storm of emotions erupted inside Tali, gushing and swelling like waves on the ocean during a storm. Why should she trust him after his lies, his manipulations, and the world of hurt, he'd dropped on her? She should push him away, throw him out of her house and out of her life. But here he was. He'd made a fool of himself in public, opened himself to her, and left himself vulnerable.

"I don't fit in your life, Leonardo." She sucked in a deep, shuddering breath. "I like who I am, and I'm not willing to change myself to become your perfect little woman." There, she'd said it.

He pulled his face away to stare into her eyes. "Did I say that I wanted you to change?"

She shook her head. He didn't say it, but he must be thinking it. He had indeed criticized her often enough.

"I don't want you to change anything, nothing. You are perfect for me."

"I'm nothing like Gianna." His ex-fiancée was the model of perfection. Excellent taste, designer clothes, perfect hair and makeup. The whole kit and caboodle. All put together in a single, gorgeous package.

"And thank goodness for that. I mean, Gianna's great, but she's not for me. I love *you, arcobaleno,* with your colorful hair, hippy clothes, kindness, sweet spirit, vocabulary, and world views. And I need your help decorating the house." He contorted his face into a grimace. "It looks like a hospital."

Was any of this real? Could she trust him when he said he loved her? Stranger things had happened. Look at her. She'd fallen in love with the exact opposite of the person she'd expected to fall in love with. If it happened to her, could it have happened to him as well?

"You do? You really want my help to decorate your house?"

Leo pulled something from the pocket of his jeans, then dropped down on one knee in front of Tali.

Was Leo doing what she thought Leo was doing? She gasped when he opened a little black velvet box and she saw a gorgeous ring. A large aquamarine diamond in the center, surrounded by a halo of marquis diamonds, all set on white gold—that was the most beautiful piece of jewelry she'd ever seen.

"Not *my* house, *our* house. I want you to decorate *our* house. I had this ring made just for you. The stone is the color of your eyes." He paused before taking a deep breath. Beads of sweat glistened on his forehead. His hand shook, still holding the little black box. "Talisman Broussard, I love you so much. Please do me the honor of becoming my wife."

He loved her! This was real. The ring, the man, the words…this wasn't a dream. Tali tried to say yes, but the word got trapped in her throat. She jumped up and down like a child. This was real and it was happening right now, right in front of her. He was smiling, still down on one knee, waiting for her answer. "Yes, oh my goodness, yes! Yes, yes, yes!"

Leo slipped the ring on Tali's finger and got back on his feet. She wrapped her arms around his waist and gave him a bright smile. "You still haven't said the words, you know."

"What words?" She knew the words he meant, but that mischievous little streak made her tease him.

"Talisman." He said her name slowly, with a hint of exasperation.

"I have to make you suffer a little, you know? But…I do love you! I love you more than life itself, Leonardo Guerranti. I love you to the moon and back."

He lifted her in the air, claiming her mouth with the possessive intimacy of a desperate lover, demanding and receiving the same fire and passion from her. How could she think there was no such thing as a soulmate? Leo was her soulmate. He'd been waiting for her in Italy since she was a little girl. Their hearts recognized each other, even if their brains took a little longer.

"Let's go home, *amore mio*. Everyone misses you there." He kissed her forehead. "The staff has been giving me the evil eye since you left. I'll send people over tomorrow to pack whatever you wish to take with you. Back home, I did some remodeling. Our dressing room is twice as big as it was, and I put all your things there. You'll have to organize them the way you like best."

He'd made room for her, even before she'd agreed to go back. She should have been upset at his arrogance, but she knew it was his way of taking care of her. Tali took Leo's arm and pulled him to the sofa with her. "Yes, let's go home. But

I'm sure they can wait an extra day." She dug her fingers under his belt and pulled on his sweater.

Leo laughed and helped her by removing the sweater and tossing it on the floor. "I aim to please." He winked as he pulled her shirt over her head. "Talisman Broussard, I love you more than you will ever know." He enveloped her in his big, strong arms.

Tali took a moment to enjoy the feeling of warmth and love. In Leo's protective embrace, she'd always be home.

Epilogue

Isola Rosalia, four years later…

Fausto and Agustina held hands and laughed, coming back from the garden. Leo's heart was light as a feather, knowing his parents were happy and in love, like a couple of teenagers.

"So this is goodbye?" Today they were returning to the yacht to continue their cruise.

"I'm afraid so, son." Fausto smiled. "My bride and I must get back to our honeymoon."

"Oh, Fausto!" Agustina pretended to pinch her husband's arm. She blushed.

Leonardo touched a button on a screen on the wall and plopped onto a large pastel-yellow sofa. "I'm afraid if I let you leave without saying goodbye to Tali, she'll never forgive me."

Agustina and Fausto sat on a plush loveseat opposite a long wooden coffee table. "We wouldn't even try." Agustina took a sweeping glance around the room. "And where is my little *nipotina*?"

"The last time I saw them, your granddaughter and her mamma were deep in Allegra's closet. They were searching for the right outfit to say goodbye to *Nonna* and *Nonno*." Leo rolled his eyes. Allegra had turned two last month, but she had Tali's sense of style. Each morning was a revelation as she sauntered downstairs for breakfast.

Bianca arrived, and Leo requested cappuccinos for his parents and himself, plus sweet tea, chocolate croissants, and a plate of *Grissini* for Tali. He laughed at the bewilderment on his parents' faces. "She says that the babies have cravings." He raised his shoulders as if that answer had to be good enough. They laughed.

"*Nonna, Nonno*!" A little tornado with ebony pigtails and big aquamarine eyes shouted as it sprinted down the stairs.

"Allegra, slow down!" A very pregnant Tali waddled down the stairs behind her unruly daughter. Leo's heartbeat picked up speed. Tali was the sexiest, most beautiful woman alive, most of all when she was pregnant. Their second and third child were coming any day now, twin girls.

Allegra jumped on the sofa between her grandparents without paying her mother any attention. She told them about how she'd picked out her little sunflower romper and Mamma helped her paint her face like a butterfly with glitter and neon paint. She told them in her two-year-old language, which was part-English, part-Italian, but most of it gibberish and anybody's guess.

Leo grabbed his daughter and lifted her in midair. "Ladies and gentlemen, I present to you *ragazza pagliaccio*." He planted a big kiss on the top of her head and spun her in the air until the little girl giggled so hard that she was out of breath.

"Leonardo, our daughter is not a clown. And if she vomits, *you'll* be cleaning it, not the staff." Tali smiled at her in-laws. "I'm sorry I took so long, but everything takes me twice as long these days." She waddled to a big, comfortable chair and dropped herself on it. "I'm hungry."

"Bianca will be here any minute with some food." Leo put Allegra on the floor and gave his wife a long, soft kiss on her mouth. He caressed her giant belly and planted a kiss there as well. Soon Allegra found one of her stuffed animals and forgot all about the adults in the room.

The refreshments arrived, and Tali dug into the plate of crispy Italian breadsticks as if her life depended on it. Leo sat back on the sofa and looked around the room. His mother congratulated Tali for her beautiful job with the living room decor. Everything was bright and welcoming.

Leo loved the year his mother had lived with them. They'd spent much time together, getting to know each other as mother and son. And with Tali there to help them through the rough times, they became very close. It pained him when Agustina decided to move out after he and Tali married. She insisted that as a newly married couple, they didn't need her as a third wheel. Fausto asked her to move in with him in his big penthouse near the Spanish Steps in Rome. Now here they were, married and on their honeymoon cruise. He loved that they'd taken a couple of days off to visit them. Tali showed signs of tiredness, so his parents said their goodbyes. This was the perfect ending to a couple of days filled with laughter, love, and food. Leo drove his parents to the village where a boat waited to take them back to their yacht.

A couple of hours later, Tali lay back on her chaise and relaxed. The terrace, with the Amalfi lemon trees and the view of the Tyrrhenian Sea, was still one of her favorite spots in the house. She might need a crane to lift her back to her feet, but she considered the reason worth the trouble. Sometimes she pinched herself to make sure she wasn't dreaming. She had a wonderful, sexy, unbelievable husband who proved his love for her every day in big and small ways. She had a sweet daughter, and soon two more would be there. The dark cloud on the horizon was Bianca's upcoming departure. She was Tali's best friend and Allegra's nanny. But Tali couldn't be selfish. Bianca was off to pursue her dream of being a chef. It had taken a lot of pleading and convincing, but the girl finally accepted having them pay for her education at one of the best culinary schools in the world. She'd spent months training another girl from the staff to be the new nanny for Allegra and the twins, but life wouldn't be the same without Bianca around every day.

"Are you brooding again because Bianca leaves for Switzerland next week?" Leo sat on the chaise next to hers.

Tali tilted her head. "Yes. I'm selfish and I'll miss her," she lamented in a dramatic voice. This was for Bianca's future, Bianca's dream. Tali ought to be delighted for her. Deep down, she was.

Leo leaned closer and caressed her forehead. "*Arcobaleno*, you are the least selfish person in the whole world. But it's okay to be human. We will all miss Bianca. I've known her since she was born. But she'll be back. And we'll go visit her, too." He moved his arm behind him and brought out a little package in a brown box. "I have something for you."

Tali grabbed the box and searched for the name of the sender. It was from her favorite gourmet shop in New Orleans. She would have jumped off her chaise and hugged Leo if her huge belly wasn't stopping her. "No way, you did not!" She ripped open the box and there they were...pralines straight from Louisiana. Nutty and sugary bits of heaven on Earth.

"Yes, I did." He held up a hand when she offered him a piece. "Uh, no, that's okay. I'm sure the babies are having cravings."

When she gave him an evil look between bites, Leo threw his head back and laughed.

Tali closed the box and put it next to her on the floor. She needed to leave room for supper. Also, Allegra would be distraught if she didn't share the delicious treats with her. The sun sank below the sea, leaving the terrace in pretty shades of dusky blue and purple.

Leo had gradually changed his schedule to work more from home or the office in Rome. Before Allegra was born, Tali went on most of his business trips. He introduced her to his world, and she thrived in it. She couldn't go with him as often after the birth of their daughter. But Leo enjoyed being a husband and a father. He chose to be a part of Allegra's daily life, and he didn't want to miss any milestones, like her first steps or words. He was devoted to their family and to Tali.

Her husband stretched his long legs on his chaise. "I have a video call with my brother later tonight."

"You'll be late to bed, I assume?"

"Yes, I'm sorry. I know how much you want to jump my bones, but you'll have to control yourself for one night." He was laughing before he could end the sentence.

"Leonardo Guerranti!" She threw a pillow at him, which he grabbed midair, avoiding a direct hit. "You little ginger-snap rascal. You're lucky I can't get out of this chaise alone."

Leonardo stood and offered Tali his hand. "Come on, *amore mio*. Let's go to our room. I'll help you take a warm bubble bath and massage your feet."

The next day it was still dark when Tali awoke with agonizing contractions in her belly and sharp pain in her lower back. The twins were on their way. She shook Leo to wake him.

As he always did at stressful times, Leo took control of the situation like a pro. They arrived at the new hospital in the village in twenty minutes. Six hours later, Leonardo held their little girls, one in each arm, and showed them to Tali. She reached out, and he placed them on her breast. Tali kissed the tops of each little head. Camilla and Caterina looked as tired as she felt, but they were perfect. Tali linked eyes with her husband. Leo was trying to hide his tears.

"I love you so much, *arcobaleno. Ti amo tantissimo!* You and our three daughters." He brushed his lips over Tali's mouth.

"I love you too, Leonardo. To the moon and back."

About the Author

Marfa Lara lives with her husband in warm and sunny South Florida, USA. She loves dogs, nature, and books. Marfa writes spicy, contemporary love stories with lively characters, fun plots, and satisfying resolutions that let the readers' imaginations run wild.

www.ingramcontent.com/pod-product-compliance
Lightning Source LLC
LaVergne TN
LVHW010103170826
845678LV00012B/2227
9781487438814